Stromboli and the Guns

by Francis Henry Gribble

STROMBOLI AND THE GUNS.

It was in the old days, when a certain famous anarchist club held its meetings in a house in one of the dismal streets abutting on the Tottenham Court Road. An evening paper had asked me to write an article about the club. An Italian waiter, whom the proprietors of a West-End *café* were protecting from the Milan police, introduced me to it as his guest; and there, in an atmosphere of pipes and lager-beer, I met Stromboli. His full name, sprawling in true cosmopolitan fashion over three languages, was Jean Antoine Stromboli Kosnapulski; but Stromboli is as much of it as I have ever been able to recall without a special effort of the memory. He was old, white-haired, white-bearded, with a furrowed brow only half hidden by his broad-brimmed, unbrushed, soft felt hat. He wore a coloured flannel shirt, with a turn-down flannel collar, showing the strong line of his throat. Beneath bushy eyebrows his eyes gleamed, keen and restless; and when I first saw him he was the centre of a group of younger revolutionists, whom he was evidently entertaining with animated reminiscences. This was the scrap of his talk that reached my ears through the hubbub—

"Yes, my comrades, it was I—*moi qui vous parle*—who made the revolution of 1848! It is not in the histories, you tell me? Then so much the worse for the histories, I answer."

" ' Yes, my comrades, it was I who made the revolution
of 1848! ' "

Stromboli and the Guns)   [*Page 8*

"'Yes, my comrades, it was I who made the revolution of 1848!'"

One naturally desired the better acquaintance of an old man who talked like that. My Milanese friend presented me to him with ceremony, as though he were introducing two rival potentates. I bowed low, with a due sense of the honour done to me, and was received with grave condescension; and then I told Stromboli that I fancied that I had heard his name before.

"In connection, if I am not mistaken," I added, "with some revolutionary movement."

Stromboli's face lighted with a smile.

Whether it was a smile of vanity, or a smile of scorn for the ignorance of the man who was not quite sure whether he had ever heard of him or not, I cannot altogether determine; but there the smile was, and it lasted through several sentences.

"It is not impossible," he said, "for I have done things—aye, and I have suffered things! I have been condemned to death by Spaniards at Santiago de

Cuba! I checked the worst excesses of the Paris Commune! And there are other stories. The revolutions, in short, have kept me very busy."

"You speak," I protested, "as though to be a revolutionist were a calling, a profession, a *métier*."

The last word seemed to please him; he smiled again as he rolled it over on his tongue.

"*Un métier? Je le crois bien.* And why not? Is there no need for 'skilled labour' in the making of a revolution? No less, I take it, than in the building of a battleship. Why, yes, then, if you choose to put it so, I am a revolutionist by *métier*."

"But still——"

The eyes flashed, and the smile changed its character.

"A poor *métier*, do you think? Then think again. It has its hazards? Granted. It is less safe than your *métier* of writing for the newspapers? Granted also. But at least it quickens the pulse and stirs the blood. At the end of it, if one is still alive, one can at least boast that one has lived. To have gambled with death in one's youth—that is something worth remembering in one's old age. And I have gambled with death wherever I could find a worthy stake to play for. If I should ever tell my stories——"

But when a man talks in that way it needs little pressure to get the stories told, and I had not pursued my acquaintance with Stromboli very far before the pressure was applied.

"*Voyons!*" he said to me one day. "I have creditors; they ask for money, a thing which I have had little leisure to amass. If there were a way of turning stories into money!"

To his astonishment I answered that with some stories, at all events, there was a way; and he forthwith told me the following, in order that the experiment might be tried. I give it in his own words, and call it—

THE GUNS OF THE DUC DE MONTPENSIER.

"Let me begin at the beginning.

"Though I am an old man, you cannot expect my memory to go further back than 1848. But it was I who made the French Revolution of that year. Without me there would have been a revolt; but it was thanks to me—it was thanks to Jean Antoine Stromboli Kosnapulski—that the revolt became a revolution.

"I was a young man in those days, twenty years old, a student at the University of Paris. I was tall, with long black hair that flowed over my collar; strong as though my muscles were of whip-cord; a swordsman who, at the *salle d'armes*, could as often as not disarm the fencing master. And when I was not studying— which was often—I talked politics in the *cafés* of the Latin quarter. There were those who said—behind my back—that I talked nonsense. They would not have dared to say it to my face; and they knew better afterwards.

"One of my comrades, however, seemed to understand me better than the others. His name was Jacques Durand; and he came to me one day with a proposal.

"'Stromboli,' he whispered in my ear. 'You know that we're trying to get up a revolution?'

"I nodded.

"'You ought to be one of us, Stromboli. You ought to join the Society of the Friends of Revolution.'

"'I never heard of that Society,' I answered.

"'That's because it's a secret society,' Jacques explained. 'You can't expect to hear about secret societies before you're asked to join them. The more secret they are the better. You can understand that, can't you?'

"Of course I could understand that.

"'I was asked to get you into it,' Jacques continued. 'A man like you——'

"One ought not, of course, to be susceptible to that sort of flattery. But one is as one is made; and I had spoken in favour of the revolution in the *cafés*. So it was agreed, and an appointment was arranged.

"'Next Sunday evening,' Jacques whispered.

"'Next Sunday evening,' I replied.

"And now picture me at this important turning point of my career. Observe me guided by my comrade through many dark and dangerous streets, where it seemed to me that a man would carry his life in his hands, unless he were, like myself, of formidable appearance. Our destination was a cellar, underneath a *café*, and we reached it by a flight of narrow, winding, slimy stairs. Jacques gave the secret signal; three slow, loud knocks upon the panel of the door, and then the humming of two lines of the Carmagnole—

'Vive le son

Du canon.'

There was a rattling of chains, and then the door was opened and we were admitted.

"'Sit down, comrade,' said one who seemed to be the President, and I took the place that had been kept vacant for me, and, as my eyes became used to the gloom, gradually surveyed the scene.

"There were some twenty of us, grouped round a plain deal table. Red flags were draped upon the damp and dripping walls. In the centre of the table was a skull, the eyes serving as the sockets of two guttering tallow candles, which were our only light. The atmosphere was misty with tobacco smoke. But the strangest thing was that almost all the comrades were personally known to me. All of them, like myself, were students at the University of Paris; and there was not a man among them whom I had ever suspected of being an earnest politician.

"But what of that? 'Still waters run deep' is your English proverb, is it not? This was, perhaps, an illustration of it. Otherwise—if that were a rude student's practical joke at the expense of the stranger who had come among —— I said to myself, 'then they shall soon learn that revolution is a subject upon which Jean Antoine Stromboli Kosnapulski does not jest.'

"But the voice of the President of the Society interrupted me.

"'The new comrade,' he said, 'will now take the oath to keep the secrets and obey the orders of the Friends of Revolution, and will drink to them in blood drawn from his own veins.'

"And I did this, a vein in my hand being opened with a penknife, and a drop let fall from it into a tumbler of red wine; and the business of the evening was proceeded with. Once more it was the President who spoke:—

"'For the benefit of the new comrade I explain the *raison d'être* of the Friends of Revolution. Our purpose is to pave the way for a revolution by removing those who are likely to be the chief obstacles to it when it comes. We choose the victim by ballot, and then we choose the executioner by ballot, so that injustice may be done to no one. I give no indications; it is not my place to give any. Some of you may think that a prince of the blood royal, now in Paris, holding high military command—— But this is your affair, not mine; the vote is secret. Vote according to your consciences.'

'We voted in solemn silence, using the President's silk hat for a ballot-urn. Seeing that I paused to think, my neighbour whispered a name into my ear. The suggestion pleased me, and I took it; and in due course the President of the assembly shuffled the papers and read them to us one by one. It was like this—

"'Montpensier, Montpensier, Montpensier, Montpensier. Comrades, the vote is unanimous for citizen the Duc de Montpensier.'

"There were loud cheers, and then there was a deadly silence. Looking round and seeing that the eyes of all were fixed intently upon me, I understood clearly what was coming next. The victim having been selected, they meant to choose me as his executioner. They thought that I should be frightened, that I should draw back, that I should give them the chance to laugh at me for talking bombast in the *cafés*. But they did not know me; they did not know Jean Antoine Stromboli Kosnapulski.

"'Comrades, I claim the work!' I cried, leaping to my feet with vigour, and so making my first appearance in any revolution. 'The choice is good,' I continued, with impetuosity. 'There could be no greater obstacle to revolution than a prince of the blood royal, who is also the commanding officer of the artillery, and would sweep the streets with his cannon when the people rise. But there is no need of any further ballot. A volunteer is better than a pressed man at any time, and I answer for Montpensier. Jean Antoine Stromboli Kosnapulski undertakes to see to it that Montpensier shall never turn his guns upon the people.'

"It was the turning of the tables on the jesters. They had brought me to this meeting-place, thinking first to terrify me by assigning me this perilous task, and then to laugh at me for my fears and my credulity in supposing that they were in earnest; and, lo! I had stood up and made them real conspirators against their will. It was their faces, instead of mine, that were now pale with terror; and their efforts to wriggle out of the responsibilities to which I had committed them were laughable.

"'It is well,' said the President; 'but a committee must now be constituted to consult with the comrade Stromboli concerning ways and means.' Which meant, of course, a committee to break it to me gently that the Friends of Revolution had made a fool of me. I repudiated the proposal with all my indignation.

"'M. le President,' I said, 'I will ask for a committee to advise me when I need advice. It was because I did not feel the need of it that I offered to execute the task. I have my plan, which I do not disclose. Within a fortnight you shall know for certain that the Duc de Montpensier will never turn his guns upon the people. In the meantime, drink to my enterprise, and then hold your peace about it.'

"Had I convinced them? Or had the power of my eye laid them under a spell? Or had my earnestness made them ashamed? I cannot say for certain. All that I know is that they rose to their feet and pledged me in the wine-cup, the toast being—

"'To the comrade who will remove Montpensier!'

"But I corrected them.

"'Drink, rather,' I said, 'to the comrade who answers for Montpensier.' And they drank.

"And now you think, perhaps, that I had some dark design to be executed with dagger, with pistol, or with poison. Perish the thought! I am not that kind of revolutionist. On the contrary, it has always been my aim to raise the tone of revolution by employing *finesse* instead of violence, wherever possible. And this time it seemed to me that *finesse* could be employed, that I could persuade the Duc de Montpensier to do my bidding, if only I could get speech with him upon a suitable occasion.

"The difficulty was, of course, to find a suitable occasion, to manage to meet the prince at some time when he was amusing himself *incognito* and unattended by his suite. All princes do these things, and it is not necessary to belong to the secret police to find out when and where. I asked Clarisse, about whom I need only tell you that she was beautiful, and that she loved me. Ah, dear Clarisse! But this is no place for sentimental memories.

"'I should not wonder,' Clarisse said, 'if he were to be at the next masked ball at the Closerie des Lilas.'

"'Eh! what?' I interrupted. 'A royal prince at a masked ball among the students?'

"'And why not, seeing that he will be masked, and no one will ever know of it who is not told?'

"There was reason in that: but a further difficulty presented itself.

"'His being there is little use to me if I cannot recognise him.' I said.

"'Perhaps I could help you,' Clarisse answered.

"'You know him, then?'

"'He does not know that I know him,' she replied.

"'But he has spoken to you?'

"She nodded laughing.

"'And would again?'

"'Perhaps?'

"'And if I were there, and watching, you would make a sign to me?'

"'I might even do that, if you were to ask me nicely.'

"So Clarisse was enlisted as my ally, though without being taken into my confidence; and I felt sure that with her help I should be able to carry out the plan that I had made.

"'We may quarrel about you, Clarisse,' was all I told her; and at that she laughed and clapped her hands.

"'That will be beautiful!' she said; for to be quarrelled about is a joy to all women when they are young and beautiful.

"Then I made other arrangements, and told my friend Jacques Durand that I should want him with me on that night.

"'You will render me,' I said, 'the help that circumstances suggest; but more than that I shall not tell you.'

"For a secret is not a secret any longer, when more than one man knows it. Time enough that Jacques should know my secret when the days had passed, and the night of the masked ball arrived.

"It came before the week was out, and there can be little need for me to tell you what it looked like. You may still see the same thing at any time in Paris, when the students are keeping carnival.

"A vast room with a polished floor, and galleries running round it, where they served refreshments; a profusion of gaily-coloured lamps suspended from the ceiling; a string band that played the tunes that set your feet dancing whether you would or no; a mob of men and girls all gaily and fantastically attired—a goodly proportion of them in masks and dominoes, and all of them, or nearly all, uproarious in their behaviour. Such was the scene through which I strode, in the garb of Mephistopheles, to answer for Montpensier.

"Jacques followed close behind me in the costume of a mediæval jester—a costume which, I allow, was scarcely appropriate to the occasion. But I had no time to think of that; for Clarisse, dressed as the Queen of Sheba, was already beckoning to me.

"'Keep near,' she whispered. 'When the time comes, I will hold up two fingers to you, thus.'

"So I kept near, and saw man after man come up, and speak to her, and go away again. My patience was sorely tried; and I began to think that she had led me on a vain chance, after all. My eyes had begun to wander about the room when Jacques recalled my attention, saying—

"'Look there, Stromboli! look!'

"I looked. A tall figure, in the guise of a Spanish Inquisitor, masked beyond all possibility of recognition, was bending down and talking to Clarisse. Her eyes caught mine, and she lifted her two fingers, giving the preconcerted signal. The hour had come.

"'Now, Jacques,' I whispered, 'I rely on you. Support me in this, and you shall see how revolutions can be helped upon their way by unexpected means.'

"'But what——'

"'Wait,' I interrupted. 'The time for explanations will come afterwards. Now is the time to act.'

"And so saying, I stepped forward and slapped my Spanish Inquisitor violently on the back.

"'What is the meaning of this, sir?' I cried angrily. 'What do you mean by insulting a lady who is here under my escort?'

"At first I thought he would have tried to strike me; but, with an effort, he restrained himself.

"'You make a mistake, sir,' he answered. 'I do not think the lady complains of having been insulted. If she does, I am quite ready to apologise to her.'

"He looked at her, as though appealing to her to say something to save the situation, and I doubt not that, being frightened, she would have said it, had I not made haste to speak again before she had time to do so.

"'You will apologise? Well and good, sir, provided that you apologise to me as well as to Madame. But an apology from a masked man is an apology that one does not accept. Take off your mask, or I shall take it off for you, and insist upon satisfaction for this insult.'

"But to unmask was, of course, the one thing that he would not do—that was what I had foreseen when I had laid this plan. And the next thing that I heard was the voice of another masked man—some courtier evidently—whispering in my ear—

"'Don't make a fool of yourself. You're talking to the Duc de Montpensier. It mustn't be known that he was here.'

"I had expected something of that sort, however, and was ready with my reply.

"'I don't believe you,' I said, with dignity. 'It is no use to romance like that with Jean Antoine Stromboli Kosnapulski. The story is the lie of a coward who dares not face the consequences of his misbehaviour.'

"Again the man approached and whispered—

"'If money is what you want to stop this row—'

"They were in such a quandary, you see, that they were ready to bribe me not to expose them. But I was a revolutionist, not a blackmailer, and this fear of exposure, thus candidly confessed, was the thing that I had relied upon to help me to my end. I took no notice of the offer, but turned again to my other masked antagonist, saying—

"'I give you your choice, sir, to unmask and apologise, or to give me satisfaction this very evening. I undertake to provide the place and the weapons. An affair of honour can be settled as well by candlelight as by daylight, and you are quite welcome to fight me with your mask on if you prefer it.'

"He was a brave man—I will do him that justice—and I had pushed him into a very awkward corner. For a minute or two he conferred in hasty whispers with his friend, and, without troubling to listen, I overheard fragments of their colloquy.

"'Mustn't let all Paris ring with this.'

"'Anything to avoid a scandal.'

10

"'Only an affair of five minutes.'

"'Teach the noisy braggart the lesson he deserves.'

"Then, when I thought the conference had lasted long enough—

"'Your decision, sir?' I demanded.

"It was the masked friend who answered, speaking very quietly—

"'Provided that we can get away from here without being followed by a crowd, we are at your service.'

"'That is easy,' said I, in the same tone. 'We have only to behave as though we were reconciled, and sit together for a minute at one of these refreshment tables.'

"'It was agreed. The crowd took no further notice of us, for little disturbances of that kind were usual enough at the Closerie des Lilas. Five minutes later the four of us were seated together in a carriage, driving to the house in which I had hired a room in readiness for this affair—a long, empty room above a shop that was for the moment without a tenant.

"The duelling-swords were there, the blinds were drawn, and the shutters closed, and a sufficiency of candles stood ready to be lighted; but one more desperate effort was made to keep the peace.

"'If my friend is willing to unmask here——'

"'He can unmask or not, as he likes,' I directed Jacques to answer; 'but I shall expect him to fight in any case.'

"'That is absolutely final?'

"'Absolutely.'

"'Very well. It is an unpleasant business. Let us make haste and get it over.'

"So lots were drawn for stations and for weapons. The lights were arranged, so far as possible, so as to favour neither of us. Still wearing our masks, but stripped of every trimming of our fancy costumes which could hinder the freedom of our movement, we advanced to the centre of the floor.

"The toss of the coin had given Jacques the direction of the combat. He made us cross our blades at the usual distance from each other, and gave the usual signal—

"'*Allez, messieurs!*'

"My antagonist could fence well. It was, no doubt, because of his skill with the small-sword that he had consented to this meeting. He meant to make it clear to me that he had spared my life, and then trust to my gratitude and my sense of honour to keep his secret. But though he was a good fencer, Jean Antoine Stromboli Kosnapulski was a better.

"You know the trick of fence which the French call *enlacer le fer*. After a cautious pass or two, I tried that, with the result that I whirled my opponent's sword out of his hand.

"'Try again, sir, when you are ready,' I said, lowering my point.

"He tried again, fighting more viciously this time, but with no more effect. Again he found himself in one corner of the room and his weapon in another.

"'Perhaps, sir, Fortune will be kinder to you the third time,' I suggested; and for the third time he advanced and faced me.

"This time I played with him longer. I took the *ligne basse*, which is always fatal, and withheld my lunge at the moment when he saw clearly, that, if I had chosen, I could have run him through. Not until nearly two minutes had elapsed did I give the quick turn of my wrist which disarmed him as before.

"Then I felt that I had sufficiently proved myself, and that the moment for my great *coup* had come.

"'Sir,' I said, bowing courteously to this proud prince, 'I honour you for your courage in this encounter with one who has the advantage over you in point of strength and skill. I could have unmasked you, or I could have killed you. Your life and your reputation have been equally at my mercy; and now I am willing to make you a free gift of both, on one condition.'

"The answer was brave enough.

"'I have asked no favour from you, sir.'

"'It is an easy condition, sir,' I continued, 'or I would not affront you by proposing it. I only ask your promise that, whatever may happen, whatever the provocation, you, as commander of the artillery, will never cause a gun to be fired upon the people of Paris.'

"He laughed. I imagine he thought he was dealing with a lunatic.

"'Is that all?' he said. 'I promise gladly. Nothing could be further from my wish than to use the guns of the French artillery against Frenchmen. Shall we now say "Good evening"?'

"He was going, but I stopped him.

"'Stay,' I said; 'it is necessary that I should have that in writing.'

"'My word, then,' he objected, 'is not enough for you?'

"'It is enough for me,' I answered; 'but I must have something to show to my friends in proof that I have executed the task which they entrusted to me. Here is the document to which I desire your signature.'

"I produced the slip of paper. These were the words upon it—

"'*I, Louis Charles, Duc de Montpensier, in consideration of my life having been spared in fair fight by Jean Antoine Stromboli Kosnapulski, do hereby engage that in no event—not even in the event of revolution—will I, as commander of the artillery, cause or permit the cannon to be used against the people.*"

"'*As witness my hand.*'

"'Now, M. le Duc,' I said, as I handed it to him, 'if you will sign this document, I pledge my word of honour that the world shall know nothing of it so long as you are faithful to the undertaking which it expresses. On the other hand, if you prefer not to sign it, I am willing to renew the combat.'

" 'If you prefer not to sign, I am willing to renew the combat '"

Stromboli and the Guns] [*Page 20*

"'If you prefer not to sign, I am willing to renew the combat.'""

"Yet again the prince stepped aside to confer with his companion. I caught odd words and phrases of their conversation—'Dangerous madman.' 'Official denial.' 'Only way out of it.' 'Avoid a scandal at all hazards.' But I affected not to hear, and waited.

"'Well, M. le Duc?' I said at last.

"He laughed again.

"'Well, well, suppose I sign? You have pen and ink there? Thank you. Even in the event of revolution? How ridiculous! As if there were any chance of another revolution in this country?'

"'Nevertheless, M. le Duc,' I answered, watching him as he wrote his name, and as both his masked friend and Jacques Durand witnessed the signature—

13

'nevertheless, M. le Duc, the wise man is he who is prepared for all emergencies.'

*　　*　　*　　*　　*

"'We saluted ceremoniously, and drove away, this time in separate carriages; and most of what remains of my story is in the history books. All the world knows that the revolution came, as I anticipated, bursting like a thunderclap in a clear sky. All the world knows that King Louis Phillipe drove away from the Tuileries in a cab, and travelled to England under the *alias* of 'Mr. Smith,' hoping, as he explained, to pass as the head of the English family of that name. But just one new thing I can tell you—a thing that I learnt afterwards from one of the royal servants, a maid who waited upon the Duchesse de Montpensier and became a good Republican after the dynasty had fallen.

"'Ah, that scene!' she said to me. 'That terrible scene! Never shall I forget it!'

"'What scene, Babette?' I asked her.

"'What scene?' she repeated, and then described it to me.

"'It was on that dreadful morning when the news came to us that Paris had, as we said, gone mad, and the people were on their way from Saint Antoine to batter down the palace gates. I was alone with the Duchess, who was crying. I was trying to console her, telling her that the police would soon take all the wicked rioters to prison; and as I did this the door opened, and who should enter, unannounced, but Queen Marie Amélie herself. Ah, she was a woman of spirit, though she was old, was Queen Marie Amélie!

"'"Where is Montpensier?" she asked, without a word of greeting.

"'It was no time for idle forms of etiquette, so the Duchess stepped to the other door of her boudoir and called down the passage, just as any common woman might.

"'A minute later M. le Duc entered. He was dressed as though for a journey, and his face was pale—I do not think I ever saw a paler face. Ignoring my presence, the Queen broke out into reproaches.

"'"Montpensier! For shame, Montpensier! Your father's throne in peril, and you strike no blow for it!"

"'If possible, his pallor deepened. Even a girl, as I was, could see that there was some struggle, which I did not understand, proceeding in his mind.

"'"What would you have me do, my mother?" he asked, trembling before her.

"'"What to do?" she repeated. "Was it for this, then, that you were given the command of the artillery—that you should tell us in the day of trouble that you don't know what to do? For shame, Montpensier! And, once more, for shame! Can't you bring out your guns and shoot this rabble down? Better to die at your post——"

"'He answered, "Anything is better, my mother, than that the French guns should be turned on the French people.'

"'"And to think that it is my own son who speaks thus to me! To think that I have lived to learn that I am the mother of a coward!"

14

"'It was clear that the taunt stung him to the quick. I thought that it must move him to take up the challenge and offer to risk his life against any odds. But no; he stood his ground and answered, with a cold, impassive stare—

"'"My mother, if I told you that I have given my plighted word to act as I am . acting, you would not believe me; but so it is. Some day, it may be, you will know the truth. In the meantime I would rather be thought a coward than know myself to be a liar."

"'"Yes, Montpensier, you are a coward! Coward—coward!" she hissed, and turned upon her heel and left him.

"'And he was a coward, wasn't he?' Babette commented. 'Even a Republican like you must think of him as a coward.'

"'No, no, Babette,' I answered; 'he was no coward. He was an honourable man who faithfully kept the pledge that had been extracted from him by Jean Antoine Stromboli Kosnapulski.'

"And then, in answer to her questions, I told her as much of the truth as it was good for her to know, and also described to her the last scene of all in this remarkable adventure.

"I now come to it. Observe!

"The populace, as you know, besieged the Tuileries, and the king and the royal family drove away in cabs. I was in the crowd, and as the Duc de Montpensier came out of the gate, I advanced a step or two to speak to him.

"'M. le Duc,' I said, "you are an honourable man, and you have kept your word. You did not use your guns against the people. Good. Accept my congratulations, and let me return to you the written undertaking which you gave me, in order that you may use it, if need be, to rehabilitate your reputation with your friends.'

"'I thank you, sir,' he answered, bowing gravely, as he took the paper from me. 'I now understand that a revolutionist may also be a man of honour.'

"He whipped up the horses and drove off, and I have never seen him since. But now you know how I made my first appearance in any revolution, and what was my meaning when I said that it was I who brought about the overthrow of the Orleanists in 1848."

THE SHORT SHRIFT OF THE FILIBUSTER.

"Voyons!" said Stromboli, as he caught me coming out of the gate of Lincoln's Inn, clutched me by the arm, and drew me into the Chancery Lane Bodega. "On the proceeds of my former story I have dined—dined sumptuously—dined several times. Think of it! Several dinners for one story! It is an advantage over the plutocracy and the *bourgeoisie* at which my heart rejoices."

"But how about the creditors?" I inquired, as we settled down at a small table in a corner.

Stromboli lit his large pipe meditatively.

"The creditors! Precisely. That is the weak point in my position. The great happiness of having money to spend caused me to forget them. Nevertheless, they still exist, and now that the money is gone they write, recalling themselves

15

to my recollection. It is unfortunate. For it seems that, even in this free country of yours, the law gives them the power to make themselves unpleasant."

I assented, and tried to explain to him the exact nature of a judgment summons, and a committal order. Then I continued—

"But you know other stories, I suppose?"

Stromboli banged the table and made the glasses ring, as he answered, half in derision, half in indignation—

"If I know other stories! He asks if I know other stories. When I tell you that I—*moi qui vous parle*—have lain under sentence of death in a Spanish prison at Santiago de Cuba, and escaped from it under circumstances which will not occur again——"

"That sounds all right," I interrupted.

"You really think so?"

"I am quite sure of it."

"Then I must make haste. The letters of the creditors begin, 'Unless——' There is evidently no time to be lost."

"There is no time like the present," I rejoined.

"Let us begin, then. And, since more money is in sight, there is no reason why I should not spend the little money that remains to me. You shall drink champagne with me, and we will smoke cigars."

And then and there, in the corner of the Bodega, while the men about us talked of the business of the Law Courts, and of the price of shares, Stromboli wafted me, in imagination, to the shores of the Pearl of the Antilles, and told me the story which I entitled—

THE SHORT SHRIFT OF THE FILIBUSTER.

"*Voyons*! Filibustering is an important branch of revolution. Though your motives be of the loftiest, yet, if the other side catch you at it, they will shoot you. The danger is the greater because you are generally on the weaker side, and therefore likely to be caught. It is a quick gamble for the heaviest of stakes. I know, for I have played the game. I have been a filibuster.

"It was in Cuba in the early seventies. The island was in revolt, and help was being sent to the rebels by the brave citizens of the United States. And one day, as I sipped my absinthe in the Café de Madrid, I was handed a telegram from New York, which ran as follows—

"'Offer you commission in Cuban Army. Start at once; begin as general. Rapid promotion if found satisfactory.'

"I thumped the table and showed the despatch to my companion.

"'To begin as general!' I cried. 'Is this a pleasantry at my expense, or is it not?'

"My companion, who was a man who had travelled widely, assured me that it was not.

"'You think,' I asked, 'that no Cuban would dare to venture upon a pleasantry with Jean Antoine Stromboli Kosnapulski?'

16

"'I am quite sure,' he answered, 'that no Cuban would spend the cost of this cablegram in doing so.'

"'Ah!'

"'Besides, you must remember that in Central American armies there is no lower commissioned rank than that of general. You are invited to begin, like other people, at the bottom of the ladder.'

"'In that case, my friend, it is not a pleasantry, but an affront. Or is it that they are afraid of exciting the jealousy of the other generals, I wonder? I must reflect.'

"I reflected in silence for at least two minutes. Then, having made up my mind, I asked my friend—

"'Do you happen to know what uniform is required by a general in the Cuban service?'

"'In the Central American armies,' my friend answered, 'every general wears the uniform that suits him best.'

"'And do you know when the next boat starts for New York?'

"'In exactly forty-eight hours from now.'

"'In that case there is no time to be lost. I will drive to the tailor's and select a uniform at once.'

"With such celerity did I form my plans. The uniform reached me just in time, neatly packed in a tin box, with my name painted on it. I dressed myself in it for the first time when I had crossed the Atlantic, and proceeded to report myself to the Cuban Junta at New York. It was an imposing uniform,—scarlet and gold lace, with a cocked hat and flaunting plumes. It caused no little admiration when, failing to find a more suitable conveyance, I rode to my destination on a tramcar. I doubt not that it would have made an even greater impression than it did if the Cuban Junta had not happened, at the moment of my call, to be represented by a Yankee.

"'Great snakes alive!' was that gentleman's first exclamation, to which I replied with dignity—

"'You are mistaken, sir. I am the new Cuban general—Jean Antoine Stromboli Kosnapulski.'

"At this he extended his hand to me cordially, continuing in the quaint language of the United States—

"'Glad to see you, General. Proud to make your acquaintance, sir. Reckon you're going to knock the sawdust out of those durned Spaniards presently. But, in the meantime, if you're in a position to put up the greenbacks, hadn't you better buy a store suit to go on with? Your present outfit, though very striking, is better adapted for dictating terms of peace upon the field of carnage than for the requirements of everyday life in New York City—the more so as there is no purpose to be served by showing our plans under the nose of the U.S. Government.'

"He was evidently a practical man—nearly all Americans are practical men— and I agreed with him that it would be easier to keep a secret in a store suit than in a uniform. It was in my store suit, therefore, that I went down according to his directions, to secure my passage to Cuba on board the paddle-steamer *Washington*. And here, once again, I found myself face to face with a practical American.

"'What is your name, sir?' he inquired, when I asked that a cabin should be retained for me, and I told him.

"'It is a name that you should know,' I said. 'I am Jean Antoine Stromboli Kosnapulski.'

"He did not seem to know me. This time, I imagine, it was my store suit that operated to my disadvantage. He answered me in the usual vernacular—

"'Seems, stranger, that's more name than there is room for in the space provided. Reckon if I enter you on this ship's books as John A. Strongboiler, that's name enough for you to sail under. Then, in case of accidents, you can say you're an American citizen, trading in cigars, and claim the protection of the Stars and Stripes.'

"He was evidently a thoroughly practical man. As a rule, it may be undignified for a general officer to disguise himself as a cigar merchant. But circumstances alter cases, and the circumstances were exceptional. So I consented, and the American shook me by the hand, saying—

"'Right, General. John A. Strongboiler doesn't need learning by heart, like the other name. And now, to show that no offence is taken, kindly name your poison.'

"So we pledged each other in a curiously concocted beverage, with plenty of powdered ice in it; and thus it was, as you see, under the strange style of John A. Strongboiler, dealer in cigars, that I sailed from New York City in the paddle-steamer *Washington* (Captain Jonathan K. Jenkins), to take up my position as a general in the Cuban Army. If I could only have foreseen! But I must not anticipate.

"We touched at Kingston, Jamaica, where we took aboard a cargo of various munitions of war, together with a number of fresh passengers—brave men, who, like myself, had enlisted as generals in the Cuban service. I invited them all to drink with me, and they did so, for it is the custom of the country. For the rest, the voyage was uneventful until the hour when our terrible catastrophe began.

"It was early, and I had left my berth to pace the deck and enjoy the fresh coolness of the morning air. Captain Jonathan K. Jenkins was there also. Through his telescope he was intently observing the movements of some craft which he evidently regarded with suspicion. Finally he closed the glass with a bang and said laconically—

"'Wal, I'm durned!'

"'What is it, Captain?' I asked, and he replied, in the American language—

"'That's a Spaniard, or I'm a Dutchman. And looking out for us. And meaning mischief. Guess, if we don't make tracks, it'll be a bad look out for all you generals.'

"'Would you like me to call a council of war, Captain?' I suggested. 'The other generals are still asleep, but——'

"He answered curtly—

"'Council of war be durned! Reckon I'm the captain of this ship, any way, and what I say goes.'

"And with that he shouted orders right and left, and altered the ship's course, and the long chase began.

"Shall I describe it? That, surely, is hardly necessary. One chase at sea is very like another. Only in this chase there were one or two moments that have specially branded themselves upon my memory.

"For hours our pursuer had gained upon us, but so slowly that we were hardly aware of his approach, and were confident of reaching a British port in safety. Then came the engineer with the terrible message—

"'Sorry, Captain, but we're just about through with the coal.'

"Never shall I forget the quick energy with which Captain Jonathan K. Jenkins confronted the emergency. He hardly seemed to be excited.

"'Wal,' he said. 'Ain't there other things that'll burn besides coal. Ain't there oil? Ain't there hams and bacon? Ain't there chairs and tables? Fling 'em in. Fling the durned ship herself into the furnaces sooner than let the engines stop.'

"We did it. I myself—Jean Antoine Stromboli Kosnapulski—worked like a common sailor, tearing up the planks and hewing down the bulwarks to supply the flames with fuel. Others, meanwhile, were busy lightening up the ship by heaving cargo overboard. Even the horses that we carried with us had to be thrown into the water. My heart bled for those poor horses as I saw their struggles; for, after all, it was a useless sacrifice. The Spaniard gained on us continually as we neared the Jamaica coast. Shots crossed our bows, warning us to surrender or be sunk.

"Then it was that a sudden uproar arose among the sailors.

"'Tain't the horses the Spaniards want. It's the Dagos. Fling them out a few Dagos and they'll stop worriting fast enough.'

"It was one of those chances that a man gets now and then of showing the metal that he is made of. The Cubans had drawn their knives; the crew were ready to rush upon them with oars and marling-spikes and every other handy weapon; Captain Jenkins had cocked his revolver and was prepared to shoot. I saw my opportunity and stepped forward to calm the tumult.

"'Captain,' I said, 'let there be no question of throwing me overboard. If you think that I can save your ship by jumping overboard, you have only to say the word and I'll do it.'

"Still overawing the mutinous sailors with the pistol, the captain gripped me by the hand.

"'Strongboiler,' he said, 'you're a gentleman, though Dagos don't run to it as a rule. But we don't do these things on board American vessels. We sink or swim together.'

19

"'Strongboiler,' he said, 'You're a gentleman.'"

Stromboli and the Guns   [Page 18

"'Strongboiler,' he said, 'You're a gentleman.'"

"And with that he gave the order to heave to, and the Spaniards boarded us. The captain greeted them with violent language.

"'What the blazes! These are British waters, ain't they? Jamaica three-mile limit. And this is the United States trading steamer, *Washington*, cleared from Kingston, Jamaica, for San Domingo. If you've got your doubts about it, look at the ship's papers and be durned!'

"'You can show your papers to the Governor, when you get to Santiago de Cuba,' was the Spanish officer's reply. 'In the meantime, you are my prisoners, and it's there that I'm going to take you.'

"He disarmed us all and put a prize crew on board; and the Spanish gunboat *Tornado* took the trading steamer *Washington* in tow, and headed straight for Santiago Harbour.

"Santiago de Cuba! To think that one of the loveliest spots upon God's earth should be given over to the abominations of these butchers!

"It was just at sunrise, on one of the loveliest mornings that I have ever known, that we made our way slowly through the narrow entrance to the bay. On either side of us low ridges of rolling hills, crowned with dark woods and verdant meadows; the bright plumage of tropical birds glancing among the trees where we hugged the shore beside the forest; here and there in the distant uplands the white walls of some country house, with the blue smoke rising like incense, untroubled by any breath of air. A scene of greater peacefulness could hardly be, save for the blue fins of the sharks that followed us, as though aware that we were journeying to our doom.

"Yet I held my head high in spite of all. Something might always happen; some chance might always show itself to the man who gave his whole mind to watching for it. Your true gambler with Death never loses hope until the hour actually comes when he must pay the forfeit.

"It seemed, however, that that hour was very near and quite inevitable. A message was conveyed to us.

"'A court-martial, for the trial of the prisoners, will sit at noon, in the *Tornado*, under the presidency of General Burriel, Governor of Santiago.' And you know what a Spanish court-martial is! It is the modern form of the Spanish Inquisition. Its purpose is not to judge, but to condemn. So that I had little hope of justice and less of mercy when my turn came to be haled before it. Only of one thing I was resolved.'

"'At least,' I said to myself, 'I will hold my head high. At least I will not beg for pity.'

"My turn came.

"Informal, but ferocious; that is how I must describe the court that sat in judgment over me. A pleasant awning was hung upon the deck. A table, with pens, ink, and paper upon it, was set for the president of the court. The other officers composing it lounged around, in a semicircle, in comfortable chairs. They drank and smoked cigarettes, and laughed gaily together, as though the sentencing of men to death were the most agreeable diversion that they knew. And I stood before them, handcuffed and guarded by marines.

"'What do you say that your name is?' was the first question put to me, and my answer was defiant.

"'It is a name that you know well enough. I am Jean Antoine Stromboli Kosnapulski.'

"For I had forgotten. The president had a list of the crew and passengers in front of him, and desired me to find my name in it. As well as my fetters would let me, I pointed, and then, when it was too late, I perceived the blunder that I had made.

"A grim and cruel smile appeared upon General Burriel's face. From the paper in front of him he read aloud the words—

"'John A. Strongboiler, dealer in cigars.' Then he pointed to me, and to the tin box, with 'Jean Antoine Stromboli Kosnapulski' painted on it, which lay upon the deck with other *pièces de conviction*, ready to be used when needed. Then he spoke slowly, with a bitter ring in his lines—

"'Untie the prisoner and let him open the box. Without doubt it is his cigar-box. If it is found to contain enough cigars to give the members of this court one hundred each, I undertake that the prisoner shall be acquitted.'

"Well, I have no surprise in store for you. You know quite well what was in the box. Under the bayonets of the marines I unpacked it defiantly; and as each article came forth—the cocked hat, the heavy boots, the scarlet tunic, the pipe-clayed breeches—the deck of the *Tornado* literally shook with shrieks of laughter. Yes, for the first and last time in my life, I, Jean Antoine Stromboli Kosnapulski was laughed at to my face.

"Perhaps for an instant the thought crossed my mind that these men would be merciful to me because I had afforded them amusement. If so, it was a thought that was dispelled with great rapidity. The members of the court-martial conferred aloud, with mocking laughter.

"'A man who travels under a false name———'

"'Talks Spanish———'

"'Says that he is an American———'

"'Though apparently a Pole———'

"'And carries a uniform about with him in a box———'

"'Which he pretends is a cigar box———'

"'Is a very interesting scoundrel———'

"'But none the less unfit to live!'

"And General Burriel summed the matter up and delivered formal sentence.

"'Prisoner, the sentence of the court upon you is that you be shot at dawn. Marines, remove the prisoner.'

"They proceeded to remove me; but before I had left the ship he called me back again.

"'Prisoner,' he said gravely, 'in consideration of the fact that you have amused the court, the court has decided upon a mitigation of your sentence.' Hope flattered me again, but only for an instant. The president continued with an evil chuckle—

"'Prisoner, the court accords you permission to put on your uniform and wear it until the hour of your execution.'

"Once more there was an outburst of uproarious merriment. My military judges held their sides in their hilarity, while the marines marched me away through jeering crowds to lodge me in the Santiago prison. They insolently made me dress myself in my uniform in their presence, and then they locked the door of my cell and left me to my reflections.

"My reflections! You may guess that these were not agreeable. Since American protection had failed me, my one hope was that, by some means or other, I might get on board the British gunboat that was lying at anchor in the harbour, and, as I had been captured in British waters, claim the protection of the Union Jack. But how to get there? That was, indeed, a problem that needed thinking out.

22

"Sitting for a space with my head buried in my hands, I thought it out in all its bearings. Presently I saw my way—or thought I saw it—and my courage and high spirits returned to me. Though I had to use a subterfuge, I would not be humble.

"I stood upon the stool, which was my only article of furniture, bringing my face level with the window through which my cell communicated with the passage, and called—

"'Gaoler! Come here, gaoler! I want you, gaoler!'

"I am aware that I spoke in the same commanding tone in which I should have summoned the boots or the waiter at an hotel. I could not help it. It is a way that I have always had, and a way that I have generally found answer. It answered in this case. The man came, growling.

"'What is the meaning of this, gaoler?' I asked curtly.

"'What is the meaning of what?' he retorted roughly.

"'Of this, gaoler—that I, a prisoner condemned to be shot at dawn, have not yet received a visit from any spiritual adviser? Even in Spain, I believe, a prisoner condemned to die has a right to spiritual consolation.' My speech, I daresay, sounded more like a reprimand than a request; but it made none the less impression upon that account. Why should it have? In all situations in life the way to secure deference is to be peremptory. My severity compelled politeness.

"'Of course, if his Excellency desires to see a priest——'

"'Certainly, gaoler,' I answered. 'Certainly I want to see a priest. And the sooner the better. Be so good as to tell one of the priests to step this way at once.'

"He had already started, when I called him back.

"'And, look here, gaoler, I'm very particular about priests. I can't accept consolation from a little priest. I must have a big one.'

"The gaoler stared at me, evidently believing that I was mad. But there was method in my madness, as you will see. I added, producing some notes from a pocket which, in their merriment over my uniform, the Spaniards had quite forgotten to search—

"'You see, my man, I'm in a position to reward you if you carry out this wish of mine.'

"He laughed an unpleasant laugh and left me. I waited with such patience as I could command, knowing that it might take some time to find a priest whose physical proportions were equal to my own. The sun had set, in fact, before the door of my cell reopened, and my gaoler, to whom I promptly handed the reward which I had promised him, ushered in a tall friar, habited in the flowing robes of the Dominican Order.

"I bowed to him with that courtesy which, I trust, has always distinguished me in dealing with my equals, even when they also happen to be my enemies.

"'I regret, my father,' I said, 'having to receive you in so unworthy an apartment. Nothing but the most stern necessity compels me.'

"The speech surprised him. He had evidently expected a more abject attitude.

"'My son, the time is short,' he answered, 'and as I doubt not that your sins are many, it were well to waste none of it in idle words.'

"I watched him intently while he spoke, and took his measure. It was important, since the success of the great *coup* that I projected depended wholly upon the nature of the man with whom I had to deal.

"He was tall, as I have said, but frail and spare of build. I read superstition in the shape of his forehead, which was high, and narrow. His thin lips, and the contour of his mouth, betokened that mixture of cruelty and weakness which has made the Spanish priest so widely hated, even in countries where there lingers no tradition of the sacred office. He was a man who would persecute if he dared. But his shifty eyes quailed before my glance, so that I felt sure that there was no real courage behind his cruelty.

"First of all, for the success of my plan, it was necessary that I should give him convincing demonstration of my superior physical powers. I made him feel the muscles of my arms.

"'There, my father,' I said to him. 'What think you of the cruelty which condemns a man in the prime of a strength like mine to be killed like a rat in a hole?'

"He was already beginning to be afraid of me, which was what I wanted; but his dignity did not yet forsake him.

"'It is the will of God,' he answered, 'and I am only here that you may make confession of your sins.'

"As he was speaking I had slowly advanced towards him. As a frightened man will, he had slunk back before me, so that I was almost pressing him against the walls in the corner of the cell farthest from the door. His eyes showed the vague terror that was coming over him. And then I said, sinking my voice to a whisper—

"'No, my father, you are not here to listen to my confession. You are here to save my life.'

"He made a movement as though he would cry for help, but with a menacing gesture I frightened him into silence, so that the sound died away, unuttered, in his throat.

"'Listen!' I went on, still in the same subdued tone of voice. 'I have made you see how strong I am. You know well that I can throttle you where you stand, long before any help can come to you. I shall do this if you make a single sound, and I shall still do it if you hesitate to obey the orders which I am about to give you. Now!'

"He made another movement, the faint beginning of a wriggle, as he thought that he might slip pass me like an eel. My hands approached his throat and he desisted. I went on—

"'It is a very simple thing that I require. In the first place, you will change clothes with me. If you are willing to do this, do not speak, but nod your head.'

"He stood there, pale and motionless, trying to find the courage to defy me.

"'My father,' I said, 'I can only give you while I count ten. One—two—three—four—five—six—seven—eight—nine——'

"He nodded.

"Undress, then,' I said. 'And mark me, if there is any noise, or any sign of hesitation——'

"This time he fully understood that I was in earnest and obeyed me. I hurried him, for there was always the chance that the gaoler might come back and interrupt us. In five minutes—or perhaps in less—the priest had put on my uniform, and I was attired in the black garb of the Dominican. But there was still one more little formality to be gone through.

"'My father,' I said, 'I might make you swear on your crucifix that you will stay here quietly until someone comes and finds you.'

"From the shifty look in his eyes I perceived that this was the very thing that he would be glad for me to do.

"'But,' I continued, 'the temptation to break your oath would be very terrible. It will be kinder not to expose you to it. So I shall gag you.'

"I improvised a gag by tearing a strip of cloth from my robes, and he submitted to have it thrust into his mouth. Then I said—

"'Good-bye, my father. In the years to come it will, perhaps, be a grateful memory to you that you have been instrumental in saving the life of Jean Antoine Stromboli Kosnapulski.'

"And with that I opened the door with the key that had been left in it for my spiritual adviser's use, and locked it again carefully behind me, and strode silently, as though deep in meditation, down the passage. No one suspected anything, no one stopped me to ask a question. The prison gate was flung open wide for me by an obsequious attendant, and I was once more at liberty. I made straight for the hills and hid myself in the woods and waited for the dawn.

"It broke at last, with all the golden grandeur of the tropics; and I found that my hiding-place, though far away, commanded a view of the yard of the very prison in which I had been confined a few short hours before. There was a bustle and confusion there. A prisoner was being dragged, struggling violently, to the place of execution. He wore a uniform—my uniform. I understood.

"'My God! The gag in his mouth! He can't explain; they've mistaken him for me; they're shooting him instead of me.'

"My heart sank and I was ashamed. Though all be fair in war, yet I had not meant this, and knew that it was unworthy of me. I give you my word that, if I had been near enough, I would have stepped forward to save the priest and resigned myself to the soldiers' vengeance. I give you my word, too, that I shouted aloud with joy when the sudden firing of cannon and pealing of alarm bells told me that the Spaniards had found out their mistake in time, and that the search for me would now, at last, begin.

"'Courage!' I said to myself, and worked my way slowly and stealthily down the hillside, meaning to strike the bay at the point where I saw the British gunboat lying at anchor close alongside.

"Before I could get to it there was a short space of open ground to be traversed, and in that open space I saw no less a person than General Burriel himself, with armed orderlies in attendance, smoking his cigar, and enjoying the fresh morning air.

"There was nothing for it but to run the gauntlet of their fire, trusting for my safety in the inaccuracy of Spanish aim. I ran; they missed me; and a minute later, with the help of a rope that a bluejacket flung to me, I had scrambled on to the deck of the *Seamew*.

"The captain seemed surprised to see me; but I explained my presence in a few hot, hurried sentences.

"'I have escaped from the Santiago prison. They took me, in the *Washington*, in British waters. I am Jean Antoine Stromboli Kosnapulski.'

"The captain rose to the occasion.

"'I don't care a hang who you are,' he replied politely, 'but if they took you in British waters, you're safe, till further notice, under the British flag.'

"And he maintained the same attitude when General Burriel himself approached and demanded my surrender, saying—

"'I want that man. That man is my prisoner.'

"The sailors had gripped their cutlasses; the marines had fixed their bayonets; and the captain of the *Seamew* stepped forward and shouted with that magnificent Anglo-Saxon insolence which is the admiration of the world—

"'Your prisoner, is he? Then, hang it, sir, let's see you come aboard my ship and take him.'

"But this the Spaniards did not do. If they had failed to keep Jean Antoine Stromboli Kosnapulski in their prison when he was alone and friendless, still less could they recapture him when the whole might of the British Empire stood behind him."

THE HUNTED POLE.

"See!" cried Stromboli, as we strolled round the Earl's Court Exhibition. "These stories of ours are becoming popular. The circulation of the magazine increases. In order to inspire my creditors with confidence, I buy a copy for each one of them. But they are many. It will be necessary to raise the price of the stories, in order that a reasonable margin of profit may remain."

I suggested that he might find editors more amenable to argument, "if, for example," I said, "you have any story of especial interest——"

As usual, Stromboli interrupted me.

"A story of especial interest! When I tell you that I have been hunted, like a wild beast, by officers of the Third Section of the Chancellerie Impériale—— "

"What! The Russian secret police?"

"Precisely."

"That ought to do."

"You think so?"

"I am sure of it."

26

"Then I will begin at once."

So we found a quiet table by the artificial lake, and while the band played valses and selections from the comic operas, Stromboli possessed himself of a vast beaker of black German beer, and blew dark clouds of smoke, and proceeded with—

THE ADVENTURE OF THE HUNTED POLE.

"*Voyons*! It must have been some twenty years ago, when the bombs were going off in Russia! There was a notion—mistaken, as it proved—that a revolution could be brought about by means of them. Fired with enthusiasm, and having an idea for a bomb of a new sort, I threw a few necessaries, including a manifesto, into my portmanteau, and started for the scene of action. But I never reached it. The machinations of the police frustrated me. Let me draw you the picture of the moment when I first learnt that the emissaries of the Third Section were on my track.

"It was at Warsaw. I had arrived there late in the afternoon, and had dined well at the best hotel, toasting the cause silently in the sparkling wine of the Widow Clicquot. After the meal I strolled out into the street to smoke my cigar, contemplatively, by moonlight.

"The hour was late. Few loiterers were abroad except myself. But presently, after I had taken several turns, I became aware of a quick, stealthy step, as of a man from nowhere, following behind me, and heard a clear but subdued voice speaking to me.

"'Whatever you do, don't look round. Walk straight on, and listen to what I say. Is your name Kosnapulski?'

"'That is part of my name,' I answered, without turning my head. 'The full name is Jean Antoine Stromboli——'

"'Right! You're the man I'm looking for,' the stranger interrupted. 'But I mustn't speak to you here. Turn up the next side street and keep in the shadow.'

"I hesitated. It might be the greeting of a comrade, or it might be the trick of a vulgar assassin. I resolved to take the risk, and turned sharply to the left, the stranger following me into the dark.

"'Don't stop,' he continued, 'and don't answer, but listen to what I say.'

"So we walked on as though we did not know each other, and he talked to me as a man speaking to himself.

"'Kosnapulski must on no account go back to his hotel. The police are there, waiting to arrest him on his return. Kosnapulski knows best whether he desires to meet them; whether there is anything compromising in his portmanteau, for example——'

"'Heavens! My manifesto!' I ejaculated. 'I've signed it in full, Jean Antoine——'

"'Hush! You mustn't speak. The manifesto must be sacrificed. The better way will be to travel on foot to the Prussian frontier. I have a little parcel here, which I am placing on a window-ledge. When I have gone, come back and fetch it. It

27

contains a few things that will help you on your way. Walk more slowly while I pass you, and then turn. Farewell!'

"He quickened his pace and glided by me—a cloaked and hooded figure. I gripped his hand silently as he passed me. It was the least—and the most—that I could do. Then I returned and found the little parcel resting in the place that he had indicated.

"I opened it in the darkest corner that I could find. It contained a false beard and a pair of spectacles, in which I disguised myself upon the spot; and a small handful of paper money, a note scrawled in pencil, which it was too dark to read; a flask of *vodki*, and a little bread and meat.

"Such was the whole of my provision for my pilgrimage. It was a terrible journey. I travelled only by night, hiding myself in the woods by day. But I need not dwell upon the details.

"My warning of peril was contained in the pencilled letter in which my mysterious friend had wrapped my bread and meat. I read it in the woods, while I was hiding in my disguise. I read it again by candle-light, in the first Prussian inn in which I found shelter after I had passed the frontier. Cheered and emboldened by generous draughts of Rhenish wine, I even went so far as to read it aloud in the *café* of the inn.

"'Listen! my comrades,' I exclaimed. 'How many of you have ever received a letter of this sort? Admire the epistolary style of those who correspond with Jean Antoine Stromboli Kosnapulski.'

"And I read—

"'Be on your guard! The Third Section means to have you. Its arm is long and it strikes unscrupulously. No country is so remote that it will not pursue you there. It will stoop to any means, even to poison and the dagger. This time I have warned you. Another time you may get no warning. If you would be safe, hide yourself until your name has been forgotten.'

"There was laughter at that, as you may guess, and a stamping of feet and a clapping of hands. I leapt upon a chair, and waved the precious missive above my head, and shouted in my exultation.

"'You see what happens. The cause prospers. Even in the Third Section itself the cause has found a friend who protects the leaders of the people.'

"They cheered me to the echo; for I was paying for the Rhenish wine. But the landlord's daughter—flaxen-haired Fräulein Minna, who was serving the refreshments—plucked me by the sleeve and signed to me to follow her. I did so.

"'Suppose,' she said, 'there were a spy of the Third Section in the *café*!'

"'Show him to me,' I replied, 'I will undertake that he leaves quickly and with no desire whatever to return.'

"'I dare not—for reasons which I must not tell you. But suppose the spy telegraphed a few words in cipher to St. Petersburg.'

"'*Eh bien*! Suppose he did. What could St. Petersburg do then?'

"'Apply for your extradition on some trumped-up charge of theft.'

"'Then are there no judges in Germany?' I asked.

"'Why, yes. But they can be bribed,' was Fräulein Minna's answer.

"'You've known that happen, little guardian angel?"

"She nodded slowly, with a look full of meaning in her eyes.

"Then I was frightened—as frightened, at least, as I have ever allowed myse to be. I began to realise the vast powers, the widespread nets, of that terrible Third Section; but I was to realise them still more vividly before many hours were over.

"At that moment her father, the landlord, burst upon the scene with noisy German oaths.

"'Thunder and lightning!' he said (among other things), while she fled in terror, before I had time to intervene.

"Then I drew myself up with dignity.

"'I must ask you to understand, sir,' I said, 'that the blame for this, if there be any blame, in wholly mine. I was merely asking your daughter a simple question which I will now address to you. Can you, at once, provide me with a horse and carriage, that I may drive to the nearest railway station?'

"The man's frown relaxed; he became comparatively civil.

"'It's a strange hour to start travelling,' he growled, 'but if you are set upon it——'

"'I am absolutely set upon it.'

"'In that case I will drive you there myself.'

"'I thank you.'

"'Come round to the stables, then.'

"He led the way, and in ten minutes or so the carriage was duly harnessed.

"'Here's something to keep you warm,' he said, offering me a flask. 'Better try to sleep a little.'

"Then he mounted the box, and drove off along the rough roads in the dark.

"The liquor in the flask was *Kirsch-wasser*—a cordial for which I had no great liking. I sipped at it and no more. Nevertheless, drowsiness overcame me, my fatigue and the previous draughts of Rhenish wine assisting, and I fell into a doze. How long I dozed I cannot tell you! All that I know is that, when I woke with a start, owing to the jolting and lurching of the carriage, the night was nearly over and the horizon tinged with the pale lemon hues that precede dawn.

"'Where in the world am I now?' I murmured to myself, with a sudden access of uneasiness.

"For the scenery that I looked upon had a strange familiarity. One after the other I recognised a hillock, a clump of trees, a group of farm-buildings—all landmarks that I had noted in my wanderings of the night before.

"'Heavens!' I ejaculated, as the whole truth flashed upon me.

"It was against her own father that the flaxen-haired Minna had wished to warn me, in the village inn; it was he, and no other, who was the spy in the pay of the Third Section. He had tried to drug me with his *Kirsch*; and his plot was

to drive me back over the frontier, before I could know what was happening, and hand me over to the police. We might cross the boundary line, for all that I could tell, at any instant. Only by immediate action could I save myself.

"Standing up in my place, and leaning forward, I gripped the man by the collar with my left hand, while with my right I drew his own revolver from his side-pocket and held it to his head.

"'Scoundrel!' I roared at him, 'pull up the horse this instant, or I'll shoot you!'

"He felt instinctively that I meant what I said, and that his game was up.

"'What is it? What have I done?' he stammered feebly, bringing the carriage to a standstill.

"Now that there was no further need for violence I recovered my customary calm.

"'You have lost your way, Herr Landlord,' I replied. 'Turn round and try to find it. Try very hard and very carefully, for this pistol of yours seems to be loaded, and might go off at the slightest provocation. Your destination, mind you, is not the Russian frontier, but the nearest German railway station.'

"He obeyed me sullenly, without further words. It was a long, long drive, over a dreary stretch of country; but it came to an end at last. At midday the weary horse jogged slowly through a village street, and I got down and paid my driver.

"'Sweep it up,' I said, scornfully tossing some coins into the gutter for him. 'That is the proper way to pay men like you. Now go and boast to your boon companions how you have driven Jean Antoine Stromboli Kosnapulski to the railway station.'

"He slunk away, fearful lest I should denounce him to the porter and the stationmaster—tall, sturdy men, who were likely to have little sympathy with a Russian spy; while I, on my part, bought my ticket and began my journey to my hiding-place.

"Do you think that it was cowardly of me to wish to hide myself? Not, surely, after my warning and my experiences of the vast powers and the vindictive malice of that great and unscrupulous organisation which was endeavouring to hunt me down. Consider! Even kings have found it necessary to hide themselves sometimes; and if a king may hide himself without loss of dignity in an oak-tree, then surely it is no shame for a revolutionist to conceal himself, for a period, in a Swiss *châlet*. The king who hid in the oak-tree would doubtless have preferred the *châlet* if he could have got to it.

"'*Reculer pour mieux sauter*,' I said to myself, 'must be my motto. I have my idea for a new bomb, and I will work it out in the friendly solitude of the pine forests.'

"So I lost no time, but journeyed day and night until I reached one of those little villages that lie high up in the hills above Montreux, on the blue waters of Lake Leman.

"These villages—Chailly, Saint Légier, and the rest—are, I should tell you, the usual hiding-places of Russian refugees. I do not say, of course, that to have a 'usual hiding-place' is the wisest course that prudence could devise. The practice,

as I now see clearly, must simplify the task of those who seek. But, at the time, I did not think of this. The shores of the Lake of Geneva seemed to me, as it were, an Alsatia where even the Third Section could not seize its victims.

"And oh! the life I lived there! It was a strange and welcome interlude of peace, to which I still sometimes look back with deep regret when I am tired.

"My *châlet* was high up, in a lonely place, on the very verge of a great pine forest. I used to rise early and wander for a mile among the meadows. Behind me towered the dark crags of the Rochers de Nave; below me gleamed the lake; before me were the black Savoy Hills, with the white dome of the Velan in the distance. The sight of these things, and of the deepening autumn tints upon the vineyards, stirred all the deep-seated poetry of my nature, until it was with difficulty that I pulled myself together, saying—

"'It is time that I was getting on with my bomb.'

"Nor was I absolutely bereft of company. In the *châlet* itself, indeed, there was no one but a deaf old woman—the widow of a woodcutter—who cooked my dinners. But, every now and again I met tourists from the Montreux hotels and entered into conversation with them. I was a mystery to them; they christened me the hermit of Saint Legier. But they invited me to refresh myself with them in the *cafés*, and I did so the more willingly that my own store of silver coin was scanty. And sometimes, when the white wine flowed, I told them stories of my revolutionary adventures, such stories as I now tell to you.

"'You do not know who I am,' I would say. 'What will you think when I tell you that I am here in hiding from the Russian secret police? Yes, so it is! I am no other than Jean Antoine Stromboli Kosnapulski.'

"And I would go on to tell them the story of my adventure in the streets of Warsaw, and other stories which I have told you, or may tell you later. It was the only return that I could make for the extensive hospitality of those knickerbockered youths.

"One day, moreover—the most memorable day of all—I made the acquaintance of a lady. Let me endeavour to recall that day.

"It was away towards Blonay, at some distance from my temporary home. She was tall and elegant, wearing a white blouse, a dark skirt, and a sailor hat; her hair was auburn; her eyes were beautifully blue. She looked about her anxiously, as though in doubt of the direction that she ought to take. Revolving the situation rapidly in my mind, I said to myself—

"'I am favourably impressed. In the absence of more serious adventure, this is emphatically an adventure to be pursued.'

"And to the lady herself I said, raising my hat with a very courteous flourish—

"'Pardon me, madam. You seem to me to have lost your way. May I place myself at your disposition and direct you?'

"From her dress and demeanour I had judged that she was English, but from her reply it appeared that she was American.

"'Now, I call that real nice of you,' was her simple answer.

"'Your destination?'

"'Way down at Territet. Grand Hôtel des Alpes.'

"'We are at some distance from the high road. You will permit me, perhaps, to guide you.'

"'I guess a white man couldn't do less,' she replied, smiling, and we strolled on together.

"Do not think me boastful or vainglorious if I tell you that, as your phrase is, I 'made the running quickly.' A revolutionist must needs do so. He is a busy man, with little leisure on his hands; he never knows what an hour may bring forth for him; gallantry is seldom possible for him, save on the condition that he makes haste with it and does not dally over the preliminaries. Besides, he enjoys advantages denied to most of you; he dazzles by virtue of the mystery which surrounds him; like the soldier, he carries his life in his hands. Such things appeal to women. It did not surprise me, therefore, that my beautiful American grew confidential.

"'I'm Daisy van Bean,' she said, 'the daughter of the railroad king, and I'm stopping with poppa at Territet. But say, now. You've walked all this way with me and you haven't yet told me what your name is.'

"It was my chance for the great *coup* which was to fascinate her imagination, if not to win her heart. I answered—

"'Beautiful Daisy, I will surprise you. I am Jean Antoine Stromboli Kosnapulski—the revolutionist—the fugitive—the inventor.'

"'The inventor? Say, now, what have you invented?'

"'I have just invented a new bomb.'

"She clapped her hands.

"'That's just too lovely for anything,' she said. 'Tell me all about it.'

"I hesitated; you would have done the same. Such secrets are not lightly to be babbled of. But was there ever an inventor who did not delight to talk of his invention—even before it was provisionally protected? So I told.

"'Beautiful Daisy, it is a bomb of which I think I have every reason to be proud. The principal ingredient is fulminate of mercury. It will make a terrible noise, but do no harm worth speaking of. You wonder; but I will explain. What is the object of a bomb? To terrorise. What is the most effective cause of terror? Noise. By noise, far more than by any other means, shall we frighten governments into conceding our demands.'

"She was not indignant, as some women would have been, but only curious.

"'I'd just love to have a look at that bomb,' she said.

"'But, beautiful Daisy,' I replied, 'even if you saw it, you would never know that it was a bomb. That is another of its merits. It can be made up to look like anything—like a cigar-case, for example, or a photograph album, or a purse.'

"'How clever!'

"'Still,' I said, 'if you would deign to accept the humble hospitality of a bachelor's roof——'

"She was emancipated—even for an American. The usual proprieties seemed to have no hold upon her.

"'I will,' she said, 'and if I'm alive to-morrow, I'll be passing here about this time.'

"And then we said good-bye. If only I had known! But I must not anticipate.

"I prepared a feast for my beautiful Daisy—such a feast as my modest means permitted. We had tea and fruits, and bread and butter, and cream, and honey—real honey, not the poisonous stuff they make at Zurich. Imagine, then, my consternation when she burst into a flood of tears, exclaiming—

"'Oh! I feel mean, I do. I feel real mean.'

"I imagined, of course, that she was ashamed of the advantage that she was taking of the confidence which her parents had reposed in her, and I tried to comfort her upon that supposition. But she was inconsolable.

"'No, no, it isn't that,' she said. 'Why I feel mean is that I deceived you. I'm not Daisy van Bean, and my poppa isn't a railroad king.'

"I tried to assure her that I was superior to all foolish prejudices about her social station; but she interrupted me again—

"'Listen! There's no time to lose. I'm just a spy and a decoy of the Third Section. They heard of you, and they sent me up to make sure, and they're following me—six of them—this very afternoon. I didn't intend telling you; but when you looked at me just then, I felt real mean.'

"'I must not stay here another moment,' I said. 'Come with me. Let us fly together.'

"'Too late! too late!' she murmured. 'I hear them coming.'

"And, sure enough, there was the sound of footsteps on the gravel. But a thought struck her.

"'What's the matter with getting out of the window?' she asked eagerly.

"'They are all barred,' I answered. 'With my own hands I fixed the bars, so that the Third Section might not break in by night. How was I to know that the Third Section would attempt to enter in broad daylight by the door?'

"She gasped.

"'Great snakes! As if, in a lonesome place like this, it wasn't the easiest thing in the world to rush the house!'

"'Rush the house!' I repeated, for the Americanism was new to me.

"But Daisy only went into hysterics on the sofa, and ten seconds later I had grasped the meaning of her words.

"The door opened and the intruders entered. There were six of them, all dressed in black, as men who go to funerals. I should have wondered at this if I had had the time to wonder, but I had none. There was no parley, no attempt at parley. They knew their *rôle* and I knew mine. I hurled the teacup at the foremost of them and gashed his forehead badly. The milk-jug followed, breaking the front teeth of the second. Then they ran in upon me and we fought at close quarters.

33

" I hurled the teacup at the foremost of them."

Stromboli and the Guns] [*Page 31*

"I hurled the teacup at the foremost of them."

"Such a fight as it was! Kicking upwards, I caught one of them under the chin, so that he lay for dead upon the floor. A second, getting the sole of my boot in the pit of his stomach, fell, doubled up, in the remotest corner of the room. A third, however, with fiendish ingenuity, hurled a chair between my legs. I tripped and fell, half dazed with the blow that my head got as I tumbled. They rushed upon me, pinioned me, and tied my hands and feet. The fight had hardly lasted a minute, and, conquered by superior numbers, I was at their mercy.

"'Run for help, Marie,' I had shouted to my old housekeeper at the beginning of the struggle, and, though she was deaf and could not hear me, what she saw sufficed to send her, screaming loudly, down the hill.

"One of my assailants, however, pursued her, caught her, put his hand over her mouth, lifted her in his arms, and brought her back and locked her in her bedroom. I saw her kicking, as he carried her past the open door, and then my senses left me.

"How long I lay stunned I cannot tell you. Wholly unconscious at first, I must have continued for hours in a state of semi-consciousness, vaguely aware, like a man in a dream, of the strange things that were going on around me. I perceived dimly that night fell and that the lamps were lighted. As it were through a mist, I saw the figures of men watching me. From time to time I heard muffled voices

34

that I could make nothing of. At last if seemed as if a cloud had suddenly lifted, and my senses returned to me with a flash.

"Horror of horrors! I was sitting—in an open coffin—with the lid lying on the floor beside it, ready to be fixed on!

"'A thousand thunders!' I yelled, trying to struggle to my feet. 'What are you doing? I am——'

"But, with my hands and feet fastened, I could scarcely move.

"A rough hand thrust me back, and one of my enemies—he with the damaged forehead—held a piece of stamped paper before my eyes, saying jeeringly—

"'You are Jean Antoine Stromboli Kosnapulski, are you? Then read that, my friend!'

"'Good Heavens!' I ejaculated.

"The paper was my *acte de décès*—my death certificate, bearing the signature—forged, of course—of the leading physician of Montreux.

"So the scheme of these ruffians of the Third Section was—to bury me alive! I could have no doubt of it, and I could do nothing to help myself. There was just a chance that Daisy might find a means of saving me; but it was a very faint chance. The others would almost certainly look too sharply after her for that. I felt my face blanch and great beads of sweat stand out upon my forehead. I made a desperate effort to free myself, but with no result.

"The men stood round and laughed at me, and then one of them advanced and clapped a pad over my mouth.

"'Here's something to keep you quiet, my friend,' he said derisively.

"Those were the last words I heard. There followed the sickly smell of chloroform, the insufferable sense of suffocation, and then a blank unconsciousness, drifting into weird and wonderful dreams. At last—after how long a period I cannot say—consciousness and recollection stole back to me together. I grasped the meaning of the incessant rattling and jolting which had been with me in my dreams, and still continued now that all my faculties were once more awakened.

"'The fiends!' I ejaculated, as the awful truth came home to me. The Third Section had kidnapped me and locked me in the coffin, for the purpose of conveying me back to Russia, where, without doubt, the hangman's rope awaited me. They had forged the death certificate in order to be able to pass the coffin, without question or investigation, through the various custom-houses. It was a better fate than being buried alive, as I had expected; but only because it gave the chapter of accidents an opening.

"'Let me out! I have no business here. I am Jean Antoine Stromboli Kosnapulski.'

"But no answer came. If any sound had issued from my narrow prison, the rumbling of the train had drowned it. If I were ever to get out of it, I must find the way myself, by my own strength and ingenuity.

"By luck my hands were not so securely fastened as they might have been. Confident in the strength of the coffin itself, my captors had evidently been guilty of carelessness in this respect. I was able to get my hands to my mouth, and, after half an hour's patient work, to undo the knot with my teeth.

"'Now let me see if they have left me any sort of tool,' I said to myself.

"So I first rescued my feet from their bonds and then fumbled in my pockets. The fools had not taken the trouble to empty them, thinking, no doubt, that it would be time enough to do this when I reached my destination; but they contained little enough, all the same. A few coins, a few notes of the Geneva Bank, a box of matches, some letters, a key, a small pocket-knife, and a cigar-case—such was the full list of the implements that I had to work with.

"'First for the cigar-case,' I mused. 'If only I knew whether that was the bomb cigar-case!'

"For I knew that, in one of my cigar-cases, I had packed one of my noisy but harmless bombs; though whether it was in the one that I had in my pocket, or in the one that I had left upon the mantelpiece, I could not recollect. In the former event my course was clear. I had only to wait until the train stopped and then fire it. The terrific din would doubtless break the drums of both my ears; the flame might even scorch my face. But at least the train would be searched after the explosion, and when smoke was seen issuing from the coffin, through the breathing-holes that had been bored for me, it would be opened.

"I waited patiently until we reached a station. Then, holding the case carefully behind my back, so as to save my face as much as possible, I jerked it open.

"But nothing happened—nothing, that is to say, except that the cigars fell out of it!

"'Let me see how far the knife will help me,' was my next idea.

"It was quite a little knife, as I have said. But the journey to the Russian frontier was a long one. I had plenty of time in front of me. It seemed just possible that, if I worked diligently, I might at least carve a hole in the lid through which I could put out a finger, if not a hand, and make a signal of distress. I opened the little pocket-knife and set to work.

"At first things went quite easily. The interior of the coffin was lined with a thick felting, designed, no doubt, to muffle any noise that its occupant might make. I worked diligently and succeeded in stripping off a patch of it. But I could get no further. Alas! and alas! Behind the padding I encountered, not wood, but solid lead, upon which the knife made no impression.

"Beaten again!'

"I gasped out the words in the bitterness of my despair and fainted. For an hour or two, as I conjecture, I lay senseless on my back. My last hope, apparently, was gone. My one chance of escaping the hangman was to die before I reached him. But then, suddenly—

"Crash! Bang!

"The noise reached me even in my leaden box. I felt the train slowing down immediately afterwards, and knew exactly what must have happened.

"'The Third Section! They stole the cigar-case from my mantelpiece. They've opened it to try the cigars and fired the bomb themselves.'

"But depression followed quickly on the heels of exultation. The firing of the bomb, though it stopped the train and caused the Russian spies to be arrested, would hardly help me to declare my presence in the coffin. The chance was that I should be left there till I starved, or else put hastily underground because no one knew who I was. What was I to do to arrest the attention of the officials, who were even now beginning to search the train from end to end.

"I thought hard, as though my brain were packed in ice, and then the inspiration came to me.

"'I have it! The cigars! If they see smoke coming through the air-holes, they'll think it was the bomb!'

"Did you ever try to smoke a cigar when you had just come round after having been under chloroform? If not, then you may take my word for it that it needs more heroism than to charge a battery or defend a barricade. I choked and coughed. I was seized by the most hideous nausea. I would have preferred the torture of the rack or thumbscrew. But I bit my lips and stuck to it, smoking for dear life's sake.

"It seemed whole weeks before my signal was discovered, though from the length of the ash upon my *Vevey fine* I knew that it could not have been more than five minutes at the outside. At last I began to hear voices, though I failed to distinguish the words, and realised that tools were at work upon my living tomb. In spite of the awful nausea, I puffed away harder than ever, pressing upwards with my hand, so as to lift the lid the very moment it was loosened.

"At last it yielded. I thrust it off, not waiting for it to be lifted, and with the stump of my cigar still between my fingers sprang to my feet, exclaiming—

"'It is time that I was out of this. I have no business here.'

"The guards and porters and policemen who were standing round turned pale, as though they had seen a ghost, and nearly fell into each other's arms.

"'Who the——' one of them ejaculated in his consternation, and I answered reassuringly—

"'Fear nothing! No harm will happen to you. I am Jean Antoine Stromboli Kosnapulski.'

"Then I stepped out of my box and looked around me. We were at Basle. On the platform I saw my old enemy of the Third Section—the same man whose forehead I had gashed—offering explanations to two policemen, who held him fast and did not seem at all disposed to listen to him.

"I pointed at him with the finger of denunciation.

"'There he is,' I cried. 'That is the culprit; that is the man who fired the bomb. He was making bombs in the woods near Montreux, and because I caught him at it he kidnapped me and threatened me with this living death. It is a voice from the dead that now convicts him of his crime.'

"You can imagine the effect that followed from my words. The crowd rushed forward as one man, vowing that it would tear the miscreant limb from limb; the police, as one man, formed up to save him for more formal and deliberate justice, and I found myself standing alone and unobserved upon the platform.

"'This is a good opportunity of retiring unobtrusively.' I said to myself. 'If I remain to give evidence, I shall be the mark of the vengeance of the Third Section for the remainder of my life. Better that an ocean should roll between us; better that I should disappear mysteriously and leave no trace behind.'

"So, taking advantage of the confusion, I bought a ticket and slipped unnoticed into the Paris train *en route* for Havre and America.

"Afterwards, from the papers, I learnt that my enemy of the Third Section— whose Government naturally could not help him—had been sentenced to imprisonment with hard labour."

THE COUNTER-REVOLUTION.

Stromboli smoked a cigar, slowly and meditatively, in my chambers. The dreamy yet earnest look in his eyes indicated that he was following an important train of thought. At last he spoke.

"What," he asked, "is your candid opinion of me as a story-teller?"

I smiled my admiration and replied—

"My friend, I find many notable qualities in your stories, but the quality which pleases me best is the modesty of the narrator."

For the first time the revolutionist flashed a suspicious glance at me, ejaculating—

"My modesty? What do you mean, then?"

"I refer," I said, "to the readiness with which you acknowledge that your appearance in revolutions has sometimes been more picturesque than dignified. Take that Nihilist story," I explained. "It seems that all that you did for the cause was to smoke a cigar in your coffin."

"But you know that my *rôle* has not often been so humble as on that occasion. If I have sunk low, I have also risen high. Listen, and I will tell you. I was once the President of a republic."

"You don't say so?" was the feeble remark I blurted out.

"I say so," he replied with gentle dignity, "for no other reason than because it happens to be the fact. I suppose I should still be the President of a republic if it had not been for the counter-revolution. A counter-revolution," he added, philosophically, "is no unusual incident in the history of the republics of Central America."

I nodded my acquiescence.

"Still," I urged, "it would be a good idea for you to tell the story. It exhibits you, no doubt, in a heroic light."

"I leave you to be the judge of that," Stromboli answered, and forthwith began upon—

THE ADVENTURE OF THE COUNTER-REVOLUTION.

"On escaping from my coffin, as I have told you, I hurried by way of Havre to New York—a city where revolutionists are treated with respect, and may even obtain municipal office by means of the Irish vote. I make no doubt I should have risen to some distinction of the kind, if another employment had not been found for me by private enterprise.

"It happened in an underground saloon bar—a 'dive' as it was called—which I frequented. I used to sit there in the company of some large-hearted Irishmen who had got into trouble with the British Government. We told each other stories of adventures, and I flatter myself that, as a story-teller, I held my own among them. But the crisis in my career arrived when I heard a strange but friendly voice at my elbow, speaking the one word—

"'Cocktail?'

"I accepted the invitation and turned round to inspect my host. As he was well-dressed, my first impression was that he was a young man of fashion—a 'dude,' in fact—engaged in seeing life. His manner, however, was not languid enough for that, and the look in his eyes was too keen.

"He watched me closely and drew to the other end of the saloon, where we could talk without being overheard. Then he jerked out—

"'Say, now! Those stories you've been tellin'—partly true, s'pose?'

"'Sir,' I said, 'if you have only offered me hospitality for the purpose of throwing doubt upon my word——'

"The stranger apologised, and, after a pause, approached the subject from a fresh point of view.

"'Say, though. You're by way of being a desperate character, anyhow, reckon?' and added, dropping the words as if what he said was of no particular importance, 'Lookin' out for employment, likely?'

"It seemed kindly meant, though crudely put; the conjecture was correct. Before I could enlarge upon the extent and nature of my qualifications he cut me short again.

"'Drop round on me at two o'clock to-morrow afternoon, and we'll fit up a deal right there. Here is my card. Now, as it's getting late, I'll say "Good-night" to you and get on the car. Glad to have made your acquaintance. Hope to renew it in the morning.'

"He shook my hand and hurried off. I examined his card and found it thus inscribed—

HIRAM P. VAN SCHUYLER,
115, Broadway.

It was a name that I knew—a name that everybody knew. Hiram P. Van Schuyler was a millionaire—a railroad king. It puzzled me to think what he could want in seeking the acquaintance of a revolutionist. Did he desire to buy me over to constitutional causes? If so——

"'There is some mystery here,' I said to myself, 'and I will probe it to the bottom.'

"So out of curiosity, rather than from any higher motive, I decided to keep the appointment which Mr. Van Schuyler had made.

"His offices occupied the whole of an enormous block of buildings; his own private room was on the highest floor. An elevator carried me up to it, a clerk showed me in, and Mr. Van Schuyler shook me warmly by the hand.

"'Glad to see you. Take a seat, Mr.——'

"'Jean Antoine Stromboli Kosnapulski,' I explained.

"'That's so. I think you were saying that you're in favour of revolutions?'

"I had not, in fact, said anything of the kind; but as he had said it for me, I replied—

"'My services—such as they are—have always been at the disposition——'

"'That's the notion, sir. Now, I'm going to make you a square offer.'

"Now, I was quite sure that he wished to bribe me to abandon my political opinions, and I prepared an appropriate reply. But I had no use for it.

"'My offer is—subject, of course, to certain conditions,' Mr. Van Schuyler continued—'to put up the dollars for a revolution in the Republic of Nicaragua.'

"Once more I breathed freely; and Mr. Van Schuyler proceeded to explain, as coolly as though he were discussing the most simple matter of business routine.

"'You see, it's this way. There are concessions to be had in Nicaragua, and I want the handling of them—concessions for railroads, concessions for gold-mining, concessions for street-lighting, and plenty more. The existing Government does not see its way to offer me sufficiently remunerative terms. Therefore, the existing Government has to go, and my nominee has to be elected President. If he can see his way to being elected Emperor, so much the better. The main thing is that, after election, he must afford me the necessary facilities for developing the resources of the country. Possibly there is no money in those resources; but that doesn't matter. There's money in the concessions, and I mean getting them. The question is, therefore: Will you accept my nomination to the Nicaraguan Presidency? Don't decide in a hurry. Think it over carefully for two minutes while I write a letter, and then let me know.'

"During the allotted interval I turned the matter over carefully in my mind.

"'Your proposal is of a somewhat unusual character,' I said.

"'If it were usual, there wouldn't be money in it,' Mr. Van Schuyler answered; and the argument impressed me favourably.

"'Then I am willing to act for you,' said I.

"'Then we'll consider it fixed up,' said he. 'Go home and draft your plan of action, and drop round again this time to-morrow. In the meantime, don't go gassing about it in the saloons, or Jacob Van Tine'll get hold of the notion and put up a rival nominee.'

"I swore that I would be as silent as the grave.

"'Right,' said Mr. Van Schuyler. 'Good afternoon, Mr.——'

"'Jean Antoine Stromboli Kosnapulski,' I prompted.

"'That is so. Good afternoon, sir.'

"So we shook hands again and I departed to mature my schemes; for there was much to be thought over and little time for thinking.

"'I will be methodical,' I said to myself, 'and begin at the beginning. First of all, I must find out where is Nicaragua, and how one gets there—whether by rail or steamer. Some further particulars as to the population, and national defences, and the present political condition of the country, will also be of service to me. They will know these things at the State Library. I will go there and inquire. But I will be careful not to divulge my secret to the librarian. Doubtless it will suffice to make him communicative if I throw out mysterious hints.'

"Then I rode down to the Library on the cars, and though I made only the most obscure references to the delicate mission with which I was entrusted, all the vast resources of the establishment were instantly placed at my disposal. In the course of a couple of hours I had probed the question to the bottom, and by the time of my next appointment with Mr. Van Schuyler was thoroughly master of my subject.

"'I have discovered,' I told him, 'that the Republic of Nicaragua contains more than a quarter of a million of inhabitants.'

"'The precise number, according to the last census, was 259,800,' said Mr. Van Schuyler. 'Fire ahead.'

"'I calculate that an army of ten thousand trustworthy volunteers——

"'Would eat up all my margin of profit and a bit more besides. Try again.'

"'I was about to say, when you interrupted me,' I proceeded, 'that such an army was obviously out of the question. On the other hands, I should have no confidence in any smaller army. Consequently——'

"'Consequently, you're going to turn up the job?'

"I drew myself up proudly in my indignation.

"'No, sir,' I replied. 'Your suggestion shows that you do not know Jean Antoine Stromboli Kosnapulski.'

"'What, then?'

"'I propose to go to Nicaragua alone, trusting to the operation of that law of Nature which, in a troubled country, invariably brings the strong man to the front.'

"Mr. Van Schuyler's face brightened.

"'Can you start right now?' he asked.

"'I can,' I answered.

"'Then I'll open you a credit of fifty thousand dollars in the bank of Nicaragua to go on with. Take another fifty thousand dollars in bills on New York, in case you need them. When you want to cable, use my private code, which I'll give you. That's all, I think.'

"It was a great undertaking, was it not, to overthrow the Government of a republic with no other weapon than my strength of character? Yet I was confident of success—so much so that, feeling that secrecy no longer mattered, I brightened my journey to San Francisco by discussing my prospects with a fellow passenger.

"He was a big, burly man, red-bearded, tanned by the sun, attired in corduroy breeches and a blue serge shirt, and he told me that he passed by the name of

Colorado Charlie. If I had desired a lieutenant to aid me in any daring enterprise, he was the very type of man I should have chosen; and as I was resolved to go alone, it seemed the most natural thing in the world to confide in him.

"'I am as brave as you are, but more cunning,' I said to him. 'Mark my words and you shall see. Like Joshua, I will blow my own trumpet, and the wall shall fall down flat. I am Jean Antoine Stromboli Kosnapulski.'

"'Stranger,' he responded cordially, 'I cotton to you. It sounds a one-sided arrangement, and rather rough on the Nicaraguans; but I take it that in the hour of victory you will be merciful as you are strong.'

"'I will,' I cried enthusiastically.

"'In that case, sir,' said Colorado Charlie, 'I will, with your permission, call for drinks, and we will lower them together in honour of your enterprise.'

"So he called for Bourbon whisky and persuaded me to drink it raw. Raw Bourbon whisky burns the throat, but comforts the stomach and unties the tongue. Until the bottle was empty I talked freely of Nicaraguan affairs. When I had finished it I fell asleep, and when I awoke I found that my companion had descended at a wayside station, leaving me alone, a sufferer from a splitting headache.

"As for the further incidents of my journey, I need not trouble you with them, for they were of no importance. There was a certain delay at San Francisco while I waited for a steamer; and the boat, when it started, travelled slowly and pitched more than I liked. Ultimately, however, I reached Managua, the capital of the country and the seat of the government which I had undertaken to overthrow with no other force than my unaided strength of character. I put up at the best hotel, where I made a favourable impression by engaging the best apartments and—contrary to my usual habit—paying for them in advance. Then I visited the bank, established my identity, furnished an example of my signature, and provided myself with a large book of cheques payable to bearer. Then I dined sumptuously, and after dinner began my campaign by summoning the landlord to my presence. In private life he was, I believe, a colonel in the army; but in his public capacity he stood before me with obsequious bows and smirks.

"'Señor Landlord,' I said to him, 'will you be kind enough to tell me the exact name of the President of this Republic?'

"He told me. It was a long name—longer even than my own—but the essential part of it was Don Juan.

"'Then, Señor Landlord,' I proceeded, 'will you kindly send a boy round to the Palace with my compliments the compliments of Jean Antoine Stromboli Kosnapulski—to say that it will give me great pleasure if the President will step round and smoke a cigar.'

"The landlord smiled, and shrugged his shoulders, and looked the picture of despair.

"'Alas! milord, it is impossible,' he answered. 'It is now three months since the President last went outside the Palace gates.'

"'How, then? Is he ill?' I asked sympathetically.

"'It is not that, milord. It is that when he shows himself, the leaders of the constitutional party shoot at him. They are bad marksmen, it is true; but the President fears that, as there are so many of them, one of them, by accident, might hit him.'

"I reflected, and, with the instinctive rapidity of genius, formed a plan.

"'In that case,' I said, 'you may inform the President that I propose to do myself the honour of calling upon him in the morning.'

"'But the President receives no one,' replied the landlord. 'It is now two months since he received anyone. When he found that so many visitors only called for the purpose of attempting to assassinate him, his Excellency decided that it would be better to give up receiving them.'

"Once more I meditated. Evidently there was a good deal of dissatisfaction felt with the existing Nicaraguan Government. The discovery quieted any qualms that might otherwise have hampered my attempt to overthrow it. It also showed me that one way of making a revolution there would be to take a side and lead it to victory; but I preferred the more manly course of independent action.

"'Then you need say nothing to the President,' I told the landlord. 'I will call upon him unannounced and take my chance of finding him.'

"'Of course milord will drive. Will four horses be sufficient for milord?' the man inquired.

"I told him I should need no horses, but should go on foot. He looked disappointed, having doubtless intended to charge me heavily for the hire of horses; but I cheered him up by writing him out a cheque payable to bearer. It was a negotiable instrument little used by Nicaraguans, and it was a part of my plan to familiarise them with the fact that the bank would hand money over the counter in exchange for them. When, early the next morning, I looked out of my window and saw my landlord in the centre of the *plaza*, attired in his military uniform, hugging a bag of silver dollars to his breast, and explaining the nature of the transaction to an animated group of fellow-citizens, my confidence in the scheme which I had devised rose high.

"'An ass laden with gold captured cities in ancient Greece,' I said to myself. 'Shall not a man carrying a cheque-book be able to do as much in modern Nicaragua?'

"I waited patiently, smoking my cigar, while the reputation of the cheque-book spread itself through the city. Then I wrote out a number of other cheques for various sums, all payable to bearer, and, putting on the evening dress and the white kid gloves which are usual for visits of ceremony, walked over to the Palace, where the President resided. As I had expected, I found the entrance barred by a couple of sentinels who were playing cards and smoking cigarettes.

"'Is the President at home?' I asked them politely.

"They sprang to their feet, thrust their cigarettes between their teeth, took up their rifles, and pointed their fixed bayonets truculently towards my stomach.

"I calmed them with a friendly gesture.

"I calmed them with a friendly gesture."

Stromboli and the Guns

"I calmed them with a friendly gesture."

"'I mean your President no harm; and, as a token of the integrity of my purpose, I would like to present you with these little cheques. You will observe that they are payable to bearer.'

"The men took the slips of pale green paper, and looked carefully at them, at me, and at each other. Smiles came out upon their faces and gradually broadened into grins. With slow and deliberate movement they leant their rifles up against the walls, and then, without a word of explanation, or even of thanks, they started together at the double for the bank.

"'It is a good beginning,' I said to myself, and walked on up the Palace garden to the front door.

"Two other sentinels were on guard here; and they also were smoking cigarettes and playing cards. To them, too, I handed cheques with a few sympathetic words, and had the satisfaction of seeing them run off, like happy children, in chase of their fellow-soldiers.

"'We are making progress,' I said to myself, and passed on unimpeded into the entrance-hall.

44

"There, various servants—first footmen in livery, and then cooks and housemaids—came out and crowded round me. I had expected it and I was prepared. The cheques to bearer, as I have told you, were already filled up and signed. It was only the work of a minute to sit down at a table, tear them out of the book, and push them into the eager, outstretched hands. The reputation of my cheques to bearer had reached them perhaps a quarter of an hour before. They snatched them from me, and, without waiting to put on their hats, men, women, and even boys, started off in rapid procession down the street towards the bank.

"Once more I was alone. But not for long. The noise made by my rapid distribution of cheques had evidently been overheard. A door opened and there issued from it a little man in a magnificent scarlet uniform, with magnificent white plumes in his cocked hat.

"'*Carramba*! Who are you, and what are you doing here?' was his ferocious greeting.

"I advanced towards him courteously.

"'I am Jean Antoine Stromboli Kosnapulski,' I answered, gently but firmly. 'May I, in my turn, inquire to whom I have the honour of speaking?'

"'*Carramba*! I am the General Montojo del Rio Grande del Norte, Minister of War to the Republic of Nicaragua,' he retorted, laying his hand upon his sword.

"In defence I laid my hand upon my cheque-book.

"'The honour is entirely mine,' I said. 'In evidence of the pleasure which I feel in making your acquaintance, you will perhaps permit me to present you with this small cheque. You will perceive that it is an open cheque for 2,000 dollars, made payable to bearer.'

"For the first time in the course of my adventure I experienced a rebuff.

"'*Carramba*!' the War Minister repeated for the third time, and flung my cheque scornfully on the floor and trampled on it, half drawing his sabre from the scabbard.

"But I was a match for him.

"'Pardon me,' I said. 'I see I have given you the wrong cheque by mistake. This was the cheque that I intended for you. It is payable to bearer, like the other, but it is for the sum of 5,000 dollars.'

"General Montojo del Rio Grande del Norte took the cheque from me and examined it; he picked up the first cheque from the floor and examined that also; Then he stuffed both cheques into his pocket and said abruptly—

"'Excuse me! I have an important appointment, and I must go and keep it.'

"And he turned on his heel with dignity and left me. A minute later I caught another glimpse of him through one of the windows. He was running—I never saw a man run so fast.

"'I think I may take it that that fixes the price of a Cabinet Minister at 5,000 dollars. The other 2,000 dollars were of the nature of a windfall which the rest will not expect.'

"Scarcely had I said it when the hall was full of Cabinet Ministers, who had apparently broken up a Cabinet Council in order to come and look for their colleague. I received them with *empressement*, and cut short their demand for explanations by the immediate production of my cheque-book. I gave cheques for 5,000 dollars each to the Minister of the Interior, the Minister for Foreign Affairs, the Finance Minister, the Minister of Education, and the Minister of Agriculture; and as they warmly shook my hand I added—

"'No doubt you would like to go and cash your cheques at once. Pray do not stand on ceremony.'

"And they did not stand; they ran. Not being in uniform, they ran, I fancy, faster even than General Montojo del Rio Grande del Norte, the War Minister himself.

"In this way, by my force of character, and my knowledge of human nature, I had at last cleared my path of obstacles. Nothing but a door now stood between me and a private interview with the President. I knocked, and was answered with the usual—

"'Come in!'

"As I had expected, the President was surprised to see me. He wore many orders and decorations; but his face had a tired and haggard look, and he shrank visibly, as though he expected me to strike him. It was an obvious relief to him when I sat down and commenced a friendly conversation.

"'Fear nothing,' I said. 'I am Jean Antoine Stromboli Kosnapulski, and I shall not assassinate you unless it is absolutely necessary.'

"Perceiving that he was at my mercy, he bowed his head with all the dignity that he could muster and waited for me to proceed.

"'I conjecture, sir,' I went on, 'that it is less for your pleasure than for your profit that you have assumed the onerous position of President of this Republic.'

"He opened his eyes wide. My candour evidently puzzled him. He did not seem to know whether to take offence at it or not.

"'If my impression is correct,' I continued, 'we have already found the basis of an arrangement which will be equally satisfactory to both of us. Do not beat about the bush, but confide in me frankly. Tell me, as nearly as you can, what the Presidency is worth to you, and I will see what sort of an offer I can make you for it.'

"His face exhibited a strange mixture of emotions, his first impulse being to ring the bell for his servants to eject me.

"'It is useless,' I explained. 'All the members of your household, and all the members of your Cabinet, have gone to the bank to cash the cheques which I have given them.'

"The President spoke for the first time.

"'Really,' he said, 'this is a very extraordinary situation.'

"'Try to realise it,' I replied, 'and avail yourself of the advantage which it offers you.'

"'I am not quite sure,' he objected, 'that I grasp your Excellency's meaning.'

46

"I explained myself in greater detail, and had the satisfaction of seeing gleams of intelligence flash in rapid succession across his features. It was my desire, I pointed out, to become President of the Nicaraguan Republic instead of him; and I was willing to pay him (in hard cash) not only reasonable, but even generous, compensation for disturbance. And I concluded, laying my hand in a friendly, and almost fatherly, fashion on his shoulder—

"'Come, now, speak to me, as between man and man. Tell me how much you are expecting to make out of it?'

"At last I had coaxed him into giving me his confidence.

"'It isn't the salary that's of importance,' he said, 'but there are certain perquisites.'

"'So I had imagined,' I interposed encouragingly.

"'I get a commission of ten per cent. on the salaries of the Cabinet Ministers; and there are other commissions—tax-collectors have to pay me for their appointments, and there's always a little something to be made by pardoning political offenders. As fast as the money comes in, I send it to London to lie as deposit in the Bank of England. On the whole, I'm doing pretty nicely, but I haven't saved enough yet. Still, it's a wearing life. There's a certain amount of discontent about; and though our social reformers aren't very good marksmen as a rule——'

"'How much?' I interrupted, for his elaborate explanations were beginning to pall upon me.

"'I think I might say 50,000 dollars,' replied the President of Nicaragua.

"To his amazement, I did not haggle, but produced New York bills for the amount and spread them on the table.

"'There,' I said. 'Now tell me what is the next step to be taken, according to the constitution of the country.'

"He took pen and ink, and a sheet of paper, and wrote something.

"'This,' he explained, 'is a decree, appointing you Provisional President during my indisposition, and announcing that there will be a *plébiscite* to elect my successor on Sunday next. In the meantime, if you cultivate the friendship of the Minister for War——'

"'Certainly. I will give him another cheque payable to bearer,' I interposed.

"'In that case he will send soldiers to see that the result of the *plébiscite* is favourable to you.'

"'And this decree?'

"'Shall be sent to the Government printers at once, and placarded in the course of half an hour. In the meantime, as I see that the members of my household are now returning from the bank, I trust that your Excellency, the Provisional President, will have lunch with me.'

"Need I say that I accepted the invitation. It was a magnificent meal, served in a large and stately dining-hall. I sat at the head of the table, with the ex-President on my right and the War Minister on my left. It was, perhaps, the supreme moment of my life—the moment when I attained the zenith of my earthly fortune. But alas for the mutability of human beings!

"We lunched at leisure like epicures, slowly enjoying the flavour of the soup, the fish, the cutlets, the poultry, and the salad. In two hours' time we had arrived at the dessert without any untoward incident; but just as we had got to the bananas and the sweet champagne, we heard the loud noise of a disturbance outside the Palace walls—a noise of firearms and of vigorous human voices.

"I looked inquiringly at the ex-President.

"'Excuse me,' he said. 'I have left my handkerchief upstairs, and I will go and fetch it.'

"He rose and vanished, and I turned to the Minister for War.

"'Your Excellency will excuse me,' he said. 'This is a matter which requires my immediate attention.'

"And he also rose and disappeared in the direction of the back door.

"So I sat alone in the great dining-hall and awaited the intruders as calmly as the Roman senators in olden times awaited the invasion of the Gauls. My arms were folded and I hugged my cheque-book to my bosom.

"The noise came nearer, there were heavy footsteps in the hall, the door burst open, and the strangers entered.

"Imagine my consternation! They were Americans—serge-shirted, corduroy-breeched desperadoes from California, and their leader was no other than my old friend, Colorado Charlie, he to whom I had confided the secret of my plans when I made his acquaintance in the train. They advanced, firing their guns as they came, picking off the glass pendants of the chandeliers, as though to keep their hands in or test their accuracy of aim. Colorado Charlie, however, signalled to them to stop, and stepped up and spoke to me, saying simply—

"'Game's up, sonnie. You've got to git.'

"I still sat on my carved mahogany chair, like the Roman senator in the story, waiting for the Gaul to pluck his beard. Colorado Charlie continued—

"'Seems you've been making a revolution for Van Schuyler. I'm here to make a revolution for Van Tine. Our methods were diverse, but our object was the same. First it was you that came out on top, and now it's me. I ain't goin' to shoot unless compelled, and if you git at once, I'll give you a free passage back to Frisco'.

"My anger was aroused, but I felt that I still held a trump card. With a flourish of my arm I drew my cheque-book and waved it in the air.

"'Let us waste no time in bandying idle words,' I said. 'I am here and I wish to stay here; but I am willing to make it worth your while to go.' For I had guessed that money, and not honour, was the object of Colorado Charlie's expedition; and his next words showed that I had guessed rightly.

"'How much, sonnie?' he asked me curtly.

"I ran my eye rapidly over the counterfoils to calculate the balance standing to my credit.

"'Sixty-one thousand two hundred and ninety-nine dollars,' I replied.

"'Right, sonnie. Hand up the draft.'

"I gave it to him and once more breathed freely. He did not hurry like the Nicaraguans, but strolled off slowly towards the bank with about a dozen members of his company. The others remained, presumably to keep an eye upon my movements. I invited them to drink my health—a thing which, otherwise, they would doubtless have done without my invitation—and promised to treat them generously as soon as I had the opportunity of cabling to New York for further funds. The idea appealed to them; they were all willing to enlist under my banner. My cup of glory and happiness was full.

"And then Colorado Charlie re-entered and dashed it from my lips.

"'It's no use, sonnie. You've got to git,' he said, handing me back my cheque.

"I protested energetically.

"'They refuse to honour my cheque?' I exclaimed. 'There is some mistake here. Come round to the bank with me and we will see the manager.'

"Without further circumlocution he blurted out the truth.

"'There ain't no manager, sonnie, and there ain't no bank. Seems you've been dealing out drafts very freely all the morning, and the holders have lost no time in cashing them. The sight of the crowd outside the bank doors created a panic among the inhabitants. They started a run on the bank for the purpose of withdrawing their deposits, and the resources were unequal to the strain.'

"'You mean to say——'

"'I mean to say that the bank is broke. The manager and the clerks have gone up country on important business, and a deputation of the leading citizens is now engaged in breaking up the premises.'

"So I perceived that I had played my trump card without result. I gasped and my head fell forward on my chest. Then I made an effort and pulled myself together. Though I had lost everything else, there was no reason why I should lose my dignity as well.

"'I bow to fate,' I said. 'I yield to circumstances. History will do justice to my memory. In the meantime, sooner than be a cause of bloodshed and dissension, I agree to abdicate.'

"'Is abdicate the same as git?' asked Colorado Charlie.

"'Is abdicate the same as git?' asked Colorado Charlie."
Stromboli and the Guns]   [Page 123

"'Is abdicate the same as git?' asked Colorado Charlie."

"I answered that the difference between the two things was immaterial; and, dipping my pen with dignity in the inkpot, I slowly wrote as follows:—

"'*In order to save my country from the unspeakable horrors of a civil war, I hereby abdicate the position of President to which I was about to be called on Sunday next by the unfettered choice of the free and independent citizens of the Republic of Nicaragua. Je ne boude pas; je me recueille.*

'*Given under my hand and seal.*

'JEAN ANTOINE STROMBOLI KOSNAPULSKI.'

"It was done. Colorado Charlie took up the paper, and read it through and expressed his satisfaction.

"'That's the notion, sonnie,' he said. 'Shake hands on it, to show there's no ill feeling'; and when I merely bowed stiffly, holding my hand behind my back, he added—

50

"'Well, never mind about that, sonnie. I understand your feelings. Anyhow, I'm going to give you a free passage back to Frisco; and if you think that 500 dollars will be of any use to you——'

"Though my pride was in revolt, I fought it down and took the money, knowing that, if I did not take it, I should land in San Francisco penniless—a contingency which it was desirable to avoid at any cost.

"And so my adventure ended—sad, yet leaving a trail of glorious memory behind it. For I had made a revolution single-handed, and enjoyed from twelve to three o'clock in the afternoon the dignity of President of a Republic."

THE MAN WITH THE ULTIMATUM.

Stromboli burst in upon me in a state of exceptional excitement. "Listen!" he cried, gesticulating energetically; and I answered that I had anticipated his wishes and was already listening.

"I have news for you," he continued.

"What news?" I asked.

"I was already telling you when you interrupted me," he replied. "I have had an idea, and with the rapidity of genius I have carried it into execution."

"What sort of idea?"

"*Voyons*! an idea that was at once brilliant and simple. Let me explain."

"By all means do so."

"Then listen! The great popularity of the stories which I have been telling you inspired me with the idea. It occurred to me, while I was occupied with my toilet, that I might profitably address a larger audience. I completed my toilet. I put on my hat. I chased an omnibus. It conveyed me to the Waterloo Road, where I descended from it."

"A strange neighbourhood to seek," I interposed.

"You think so? But I had my plan. I descended from the omnibus at a door whereupon was a brass plate bearing the words, 'Musical and Dramatic Agent.'"

"Heavens!" I ejaculated, beginning to understand, and Stromboli proceeded—

"The door was open, and I walked in. I found myself in an antechamber, surrounded by men with blue chins, and young women with blue eyes and fair hair, who stared at me curiously. I took no more notice of them than if they had been waxwork models, but walked on to another door, leading to an inner room. A young man—a clerk of some kind—presumed to bar my progress. I swept him before me and so forced my passage into the presence of the 'Dramatic and Musical Agent.'"

"I presume," I said, "that the 'Dramatic and Musical Agent' was surprised to see you."

"Naturally. 'Who the dickens are you, sir?' was his brusque but kindly greeting. 'Who should I be but Jean Antoine Stromboli Kosnapulski?' I replied. 'What do you want here?' he asked inquisitively. 'I am here to do business with you to our mutual advantage,' I explained. And with that I sat down affably in his arm-chair and engaged him in a serious conversation."

51

"What!" I explained. "You don't mean to tell me that you are going on the music-halls in the character of a performing Revolutionist?"

Stromboli seemed hurt.

"It has been arranged," he said, "that I am to give a series of lectures on my experiences at certain Palaces of Varieties. The general title of the series is to be, 'Disturbances that I have Made.' It is not precisely what I contemplated in my youth; but it is a way, like another, of making provision for my age."

"Precisely," I said, seeing that it was useless to argue with him. "With which of your thrilling experiences are you meaning to begin?"

"With a certain further experience of a Central American republic," Stromboli answered.

"Your exploits in that quarter of the world do not seem to have been of a very satisfactory character," I objected.

"I certainly had my ups and downs there," Stromboli admitted. "Central America is a place where the unexpected happens on the smallest provocation. But that, I take it, is no disadvantage from the story-teller's point of view."

I frankly allowed that it was not.

"Then I will tell my new audiences," said Stromboli, "how I once acted, in Central America, in the capacity of a diplomatic representative of Her Britannic Majesty."

"Good," said I. "Will you rehearse the lecture now?"

"It is for that very purpose that I have come to see you," said Stromboli.

"Proceed," said I, and he proceeded with

THE ADVENTURE OF THE MAN WITH THE ULTIMATUM.

"It has to be admitted—it has been admitted—that my experiences as President of the Republic of Nicaragua were not entirely to my satisfaction. It was also easy for me to perceive that they were likely to entail a coolness between myself and the confiding capitalist whose money I had spent—a thing to be avoided if I hoped to have the spending of more of his money at some future time.

"'This must not be,' I said to myself. 'Something must turn up—if not in Nicaragua, then elsewhere. There are other Central American republics besides Nicaragua, and in all of them the career is open to the talents. But the adventure in which I next engage must not be one involving the outlay of large sums of ready money, seeing that five hundred dollars is my present worldly wealth.'

"Even as I was soliloquising, my opportunity occurred. Without immodesty I may take some credit to myself for having recognised that opportunity at a glance. The man who introduced it to my notice did not; but, as I required his help, I soon explained it to him.

"His name was Captain Shagg—which, when you come to think of it, is every bit as good a name as Cavendish—and he commanded the little trading steamer on which Colorado Charlie had given me my free passage back to San Francisco. Hardly had we cleared Managua Harbour than he began to beguile the time by passing criticisms on Central American republics generally.

"'They're lively places, sir, lively places. They may not be caught in the great whirlpool of European complications; but they don't stagnate, sir, they don't stagnate. If anyone was to come alongside and ask them to stagnate, I sort of reckon they'd say they'd see him hanged first. Here in Nicaragua they seem to be raising Cain with the generous help of imported Amurrican citizens. Over in Salvador, from what they tell me, they're raising Cain by their own individual efforts.'

"'This is very interesting,' I said. 'What's happening in San Salvador?'

"'A revolution, sir—with trimmings.'

"'With what?' I repeated.

"'With trimmings, sir. And when I say trimmings, I mean shootings. And I also mean destruction of property and outrages on British and Amurrican subjects.'

"'Did you hear the story in any detail, captain?' I inquired.

"'Detail, sir? Yards of it, from a dago employed in the Amurrican Consulate, who deserted his duties and came along here because he was peaceably inclined. He told me that the American Consul was all right, having started for his annual holiday just before the bust up began, but the British Vice-Consul had his house wrecked and escaped to the mountains in his nightshirt. He was only a dago, so I suppose the other dagos thought they could do what they liked with him.'

"'And has the British Navy no word to say?' I interposed, and Captain Shagg replied reflectively.

"'Wal,' he said, 'I guess there'll be a tea party, not to say a picnic, when the British Navy comes along. But it ain't there yet, and in the meantime the dago in the nightshirt will be taking cold. Strange as it may seem, the Pacific Squadron is not permanently stationed off the coast of Salvador."

"The outlines of my scheme had already begun to sketch themselves in my brain.

"'I'll put another question to you, captain,' I said. 'A well-informed man like yourself might know where the nearest British cruiser or gunboat is, and how soon it is likely to arrive.'

"Captain Shagg mopped his brow and spat upon the deck, as is the habit of American seafarers when engaged in thought.

"'So far as I know,' he answered, 'the nearest British gunboat is way down off Colombia. When it arrives at Libertad will nat'rally depend upon when it starts. Anyhow, I reckon it won't come alongside quite so soon as the dago in the nightshirt would like to see it. And I also reckon that dago wants to see it just as badly as he ever wanted to see anything.'

"'You think it likely, then,' I continued, 'that we shall be off Libertad before the gunboat?'

"'Why, certainly,' said Captain Shagg.

"Then I was able to fill in the outlines of my scheme.

"'*Voyons*!' I said, 'the voice of duty calls. It would be possible, I take it, to make such alterations in the appearance of this steamer as would cause it to be mistaken for a gunboat by persons whose acquaintance with gunboats was not particularly extensive?'

"The captain spat again on the deck. He also half closed one of his eyes and concentrated the other upon me.

"'Stranger,' he said, 'I reckon that you did not put that question to me merely out of idle curiosity.'

"I half closed one of my own eyes, and admitted that I had been actuated by a higher motive.

"'You have a notion, likely?' he continued.

"'I do not waste words,' I rejoined impatiently. 'I do not talk for the sake of talking. I am Jean Antoine——'

"'Jest so,' said Captain Shagg. 'You have a notion. I have no notions myself, but I have grit. And I'm a judge of notions—more particularly over a glass of rum. The rum, stranger, is in my cabin.'

"He led the way to his cabin, and I followed him. He produced the rum, and would not let me follow up the subject until we had both drunk two stiff glasses of it, explaining that, for a proper appreciation of notions a clear head was necessary. Then, having filled the glasses for the third time, he got to business.

"'Now, stranger, what is your notion?' he inquired encouragingly.

"I answered by repeating my previous question—

"'I must first know whether you can do anything to this steamer to make it pass, at a reasonable distance, and among comparatively ignorant people, for a gunboat.'

"'Wal, yes,' said Captain Shagg. 'There's Union Jacks; there's paint; there's timber to make dummy guns. Allowing that it was worth while, I reckon it could be done. But what's your notion, stranger?'

"I explained that my notion was that we should disguise the trading steamer as a gunboat, fly the Union Jack, and proceed to the port of Libertad as the plenipotentiary representatives of the British Government.

"Captain Shagg tossed off his glass of rum and shook hands with me in his enthusiasm. "'*And* bring off the dago in the nightshirt? *And* arrest the President? *And* drill a hole in him if he argues? Sir, your notion is equally creditable to your heart and to your head. Sir, it appeals to my chivalrous instincts as an Amurrican citizen. Sir, I tumble.'

"I was not positive that he had caught my meaning quite so completely as he fancied. For, as you shall see, the rescue of the British Vice-Consul was not the only object that I had in view As I had secured his co-operation, however, it seemed superfluous to puzzle him with further details, lest he should raise objections. It would be better, I felt, to spring those details on him later, when there was no time for argument. In the meantime we had plenty to do in deciding how certain obvious obstacles should be overcome.

"First of all, I suggested, there were the feelings of the crew to be considered; but it appeared that this difficulty was not serious.

"'You leave the crew to me, stranger,' said Captain Shagg. 'They're spoiling for a fight, every man of them; and if they weren't, I'd put a sense of dooty into them till they were.'

"Thus reassured, I lifted my hat and bowed in homage to this terrible disciplinarian. He acknowledged the compliment by filling up my glass, and then raised an objection of his own.

"'Those dagos aren't very spry, he said, 'but they aren't absolute durned fools, either, and it's more than likely they'll expect us to show some sort of papers, just by way of proving who we are, more especially as you yourself, if I may say so, look more like a Smoky Mountain prophet than a British naval officer.'

"This time it was my turn to acknowledge a compliment and reassure the captain.

"'What can have led you to imagine that I propose to figure in the ridiculous light of an ambassador without credentials? It would be too absurd. Of course we shall present credentials.'

"'Wal, we ain't got the real thing aboard this ship, anyhow, I reckon,' said Captain Shagg; and his stupidity amazed me.

"'Do you imagine that the newly elected provisional President of the Republic of Salvador would be likely to recognise the real thing if it were shown to him?' I retorted.

"Maybe not,' said the captain, cautiously. 'But I'd guess it's likely there'd be somebody mouching around who'd recognise the substitute.'

"'You think so?'

"'Wal, why no? There's the ship's papers—they'd know those. There's the log-book—they'd know that. There's my master's certificate—that won't flummox 'em, either.'

"He was apparently intending to recite the complete list of more or less official documents on board his vessel; but I interrupted him impatiently, drawing a document from my own pocket.

"'No doubt they would know those documents,' I said. 'No doubt they would also recognise your Post Office Savings Bank book, and your marriage settlement, and your receipts for harbour dues, and your tailor's bills, if those are documents which you are in the habit of carrying about with you. But do you suppose the average newly elected provisional President of the Republic of Salvador is likely to recognise this?'

"And I unfolded my paper, which was mounted on canvas, and read with solemn emphasis—

"*Dieu et Mon Droit.*

"*We, John, Earl of Kimberley, Baron Wodehouse, a Peer of the United Kingdom of Great Britain and Ireland, and a Baronet, a Member of Her Britannic Majesty's Most Honourable Privy Council, a Knight of the Most Noble Order of the Garter, Her Majesty's Principal Secretary of State for Foreign Affairs, etc., etc., etc.*

55

"Request and require in the name of Her Majesty all those whom it may concern to allow Jean Antoine Stromboli Kosnapulski (British subject) travelling on the Continent to pass freely without let or hindrance and to afford him every assistance and protection of which he may stand in need.

"Given at the Foreign Office, London.

"The American skipper listened and was visibly impressed. It looked as though his eyeballs would start from their sockets in his astonishment. He banged the cabin table with his first, exclaiming—

"'Snakes alive, man! that is the real thing, ain't it?'

"I explained that it was merely an ordinary Foreign Office passport, which I had acquired through my banker when, for a brief period, I had a bank account in London; but Captain Shagg was not disheartened.

"'Wal,' he said, 'it bluffed me, anyhow. And I conclude that what is good enough to bluff me is good enough to bluff the dagos. I'm with you, stranger, in your gallant enterprise. Full speed ahead!'

"I further pointed out that, in order to carry conviction to the eye as well as to the ear, the credentials of an envoy extraordinary and minister plenipotentiary must be tied up in green ribbon and fastened with green sealing-wax; and Captain Shagg, with the natural adroitness of the sailor man, showed me how this could be managed.

"'I have no ribbon,' he said, 'but I can make some out of the lining of my hat. I have no green sealing-wax, but I have plenty of green paint. It won't be the real thing, any more than the papers are, but it will be near enough for the dagos. And now we'll pipe all hands on deck and tell the crew just what it's needful they should know."

"So, our plan being arranged, the preparations for carrying it through were set in hand at once. We hove to in mid-ocean and gave the ship a new coating of black paint; we holystoned the deck: we smartened up the vessel's rig; we painted some spare spars and fixed up dummy guns; we lettered H.M.S. *Terror* on the caps of the crew of the gig; and we hoisted the Union Jack conspicuously.

"The result was satisfactory. I do not say we could have stood inspection by an admiral; but there was no admiral to inspect us. Captain Shagg, at any rate, was gratified and confident.

"'Tain't the real thing,' he repeated, 'but it's near enough to bluff the dagos. No dago will express doubts as to the genuineness of this show—more especially when he observes that my hand is deep down in my revolver pocket.'

"And he added, summing up the situation generally—

"'The proceedings may not be precisely regular, but they are regular enough for dagos. On an errand of mercy, for the purpose of rescuing a poor cuss catching cold on the hillside in his nightshirt, other considerations besides those of regularity must be weighed. I stand in with you, sir, in this enterprise, which, as I have remarked, does equal credit to your heart and to your head: and if, as I venture to anticipate, the British Government rewards you for your noble conduct, I look to stand in with you in that little matter also.'

"For Captain Shagg, as I have hinted, was less quick-witted than myself. He had not yet gathered in what manner I proposed to make the adventure profitable, and I did not think it necessary to inform him before the hour for taking profits came.

"As we conversed, however, we were quickly nearing the Port of Libertad, and the hour for stirring action was at hand.

"Steaming slowly, we selected a point of vantage from which, if our guns had been real guns, we could readily have shelled all the principal public buildings of the town—yet so far out that we could not be too critically examined. Then we manned a boat with the most presentable of our sailors and rowed ashore.

"'You do the palavering, stranger,' said Captain Shagg. 'When the shooting begins, I'll take a hand. I may not have the distinguished manners of an ambassador, but I am uncommonly quick on the draw.'

"'You have only to put your trust in me, and there will be no need for you to shoot,' I replied.

"'Shooting is a language that goes without the need of an interpreter,' Captain Shagg protested.

"'So is my Spanish,' I answered proudly.

"'Go ahead, then!' said the captain; and we went ahead.

"A courteous official in a ragged uniform received us on the quay. He represented the Custom-house, and inquired whether we had anything to declare.

"'Better shoot now, hadn't I, just to clear the air a bit?' whispered the captain under his breath; but I checked his enthusiasm with an authoritative gesture and explained the situation to the Custom-house official.

"The sight of the passport, with its green ribbon and green paint, impressed him as we had expected. He bowed like a footman and said he would summon a guard of honour to conduct us to the presence of the President. While we awaited the arrival of the guard of honour I conversed with him, in order to inform myself of the precise position of affairs.

"'I understand,' I said gravely, 'that there has lately been a change in the *personnel* of your Executive. Be good enough to tell me exactly what has happened.'

"He told me, supplementing the story which I had heard from Captain Shagg. There had been a revolution—as I knew. A President named Gomez had been succeeded by a President named Gonzalez. As the President named Gomez had shown some reluctance to retire, the President named Gonzalez had been obliged to have him stood against a wall and shot. There had been other rioting, but order was now restored. The President named Gonzalez would unquestionably be very happy to receive the accredited representative of Her Britannic Majesty's Government, and regard it as a specially fortunate occurrence that he happened to be at Libertad at the moment of our arrival, so that he could see us there, without troubling us to travel to San Salvador.

"'The pleasure will be mutual,' I replied politely; and I had hardly made my answer before the guard of honour came.

"It consisted of ten ragged soldiers smoking cigarettes, and an officer, with plenty of tattered gold braid, smoking a Mexican cheroot. I showed the officer my embellished passport. He examined the outside of it, and, being satisfied that it was in order, introduced himself.

"'I am Colonel Sombrero, of the President's bodyguard.' he said. 'If your Excellency will do me the great honour of accepting a cigar——' I took one. Captain Shagg said that he preferred a pipe, and lighted up. The colonel seemed surprised at his choice, but shrugged his shoulders in a friendly manner, making allowance for the peculiar tastes of foreigners. He also said he was sorry we had not announced our intention of visiting the President, as in that case there would have been a carriage waiting for us. In reply, I said that we were willing to dispense with ceremony, because our business was of a pressing character. 'In that case,' said Colonel Sombrero, 'may I venture to invite your Excellencies to be so infinitely condescending as to ride with me to the Plaza in a tramcar.'

"'A tramcar drawn by mules,' I answered, 'is a somewhat unusual conveyance for an ambassador; but, our business being urgent, we will waive the point.'

"So we got into the car with the officer, while the men stationed themselves on the platform beside the driver, and rattled through the streets.

"It was only a ten minutes' ride. Looking out of the window as we jolted along we saw many signs of the recent disturbances; wrecked houses, pillaged shops, and here and there a dead body being removed for burial. But the disturbances themselves were over; we had been correctly informed that order was restored.

"A few minutes later we were ushered into the presence of the man who had restored it. He was a civilian, some five feet high, dressed in a frock-coat that did not fit him, and a pair of shabby trousers that had seen better days; his collar and tie testified to a toilet made in our honour. The expression of his face was not devoid of vigour, but cunning was even more prominently marked upon it. I towered conspicuously above him.

"'Attention!' called the colonel to his men, and they arranged themselves in rows on the two sides of the hall, still smoking cigarettes—to smoke on duty being, as I am told, the privilege of the soldiers in all the Central American republics.

"President Gonzalez and I bowed to each other with distinguished courtesy; Captain Shagg also bowed after the usual careless fashion of a seafaring man. The colonel pulled at his cheroot; the soldiers puffed their cigarettes; and I proceeded to my business without delay.

"'Here is the letter accrediting me to the Government of your Excellency,' I said. 'If your Excellency does not read English——'

"To my relief he shook his head.

"'Your Excellency will at least recognise the British arms, and the sign manual of the British Minister for Foreign Affairs.'

"His Excellency bowed again. He said he always had been and always should be animated by the most friendly sentiments towards Her Britannic Majesty's Government; and as he said this he handed me back my passport, which I thrust into my pocket.

58

"'Your Excellency,' I proceeded, affably but firmly, 'has now an opportunity for demonstrating the genuineness of those amicable sentiments.'

"He made a gesture as though to signify that his entire possessions were at Her Britannic Majesty's disposal.

"'The object of my mission,' I continued, 'is to draw the attention of your Excellency to an outrage committed upon the person of Her Britannic Majesty's Vice-Consul, and to require immediate satisfaction.'

"To my amazement the President was not at all embarrassed. He smiled on me more graciously than ever.

"'The outrage to which you refer,' he said, 'was committed by the party of the President whom I have succeeded. I am happy to inform you that ex-President Gomez has already paid the penalty of his crime; and your Vice-Consul—a gentleman for whom I personally have a great affection and respect—is now reinstated in his honourable office.'

"It was not what I had expected; and Captain Shagg, to whom I interpreted the speech, was absolutely dumfoundered by the turn affairs were taking.

"'Why, durn,' he said, 'this dago's a white man, after all. We've come on a fool's errand, and the sooner we quit, the better for our health. Else he'll fetch the other dago along, and the game'll be blown upon, and we'll have to start the shooting without the moral support of a clear conscience.'

"I checked him, however, and introduced the necessary modification into my plan.

"'Captain,' I said, 'it was arranged, I think, that it was I who was to take control of the details of this piece of business.'

"And to the President I replied—

"'Your Excellency must understand that my instructions require me to verify your Excellency's statement.'

"'Naturally,' he answered, with more gracious affability than ever.

"'It is necessary that I should see and speak with our Vice-Consul.'

"'Naturally. He shall be fetched.

"'It will be necessary for me to speak with him in private.'

"'By all means. A room will be placed at your disposition.'

"'And, after the interview, it will be desirable that I should speak with your Excellency again.'

"'You will add to the favour for which I am already indebted to you by doing so.'

"The man's politeness was absolutely irritating. To Captain Shagg it seemed to foreshadow danger.

"'Now what's this fool-game, stranger?' he protested.

"'Wait,' I answered; 'the game is not finished yet.'

"For, as I have said already, this captain was a dull-witted though a determined man.

"My calm words quieted him, however; he waited patiently, with his eye on the President, and his hand in his revolver pocket, while I conversed apart with the Vice-Consul, and took him, as far as was necessary, into my confidence.

"It would be superfluous to report our rapid dialogue; it is enough to give the Vice-Consul's answer to my arguments.

"'Señor,' he said, 'President Gonzalez is my friend. But justice is more to me than friendship—especially as I am a poor man with expensive tastes.'

"Strange words, you think? Their meaning will be clear enough when I relate what happened at my second interview with the President of the Republic.

"'Your Excellency,' I said, returning with the Vice-Consul by my side, 'I have the honour to inform you that I have now completed my inquiries, and can give you my decision in the matter.'

"His Excellency bowed and showed his white teeth smilingly. The soldiers stood at attention, lighting fresh cigarettes from the stumps of the old ones as they did so. And then I showed my hand, and, so to say, threw my bombshell.

"'The personal behaviour of your Excellency in connection with the unfortunate *contretemps* which has brought me here has been beyond all praise. I have the honour to thank your Excellency in the name of Her Britannic Majesty.'

"There was another bow and a fresh display of gleaming teeth.

"'But,' I continued, 'I have the honour to address your Excellency at the present moment, not as private individual, but as the representative of the State. It must be obvious to your Excellency that, in a civilised country like the Republic of Salvador, the responsibility for an outrage that has been perpetrated does not disappear in consequence of a change of Government. Changes of Government are too frequent in the Republic of Salvador for that political doctrine to be accepted, even by the representative of a friendly Power. On the contrary, the liability remains, and the indemnity must still be paid. In consideration, however, of the correct behaviour of your Excellency in the matter, I am prepared to fix that indemnity at the very moderate sum of 50,000 dollars.'

"A word or two whispered in his ear by the Vice-Consul had caused Captain Shagg to listen carefully to my speech. He did not understand much of it, but he caught the essential words, '50,000 dollars,' and his dull intelligence at last grasped the true nature of the business which he was assisting me to carry through. He went so far as to withdraw his hand from his revolver pocket and slap his thigh, exclaiming—

"'Bully for you, stranger! You're a dandy! Durned if I ever guessed——'

"'Hush!' I said, fearing lest his strange manners should arouse suspicion; and he stopped and put his hand back into his revolver pocket in readiness for emergencies, while I turned to the President, saying, 'Your Excellency's reply?'

"He shrugged his shoulders, laughed, pretended to think that I was joking with him. I went on sternly—

"'Your Excellency must understand that, though I speak in the polished phrases of diplomatic intercourse, my demand is, in fact, of the nature of an ultimatum, failure to comply with which will entail a rupture of amicable relations.'

"Not knowing what else to say, the President said that the rupture of friendly relations would be painful to him.

"'It will be the more painful,' I said, pointing through the open window to where our steamer flew the Union Jack. 'It will be the more painful in that its first consequence will be the bombardment of this port, and the destruction of all the public buildings.'

"For the first time in the course of the interview the President began to show his temper.

"'It might also result,' he said, 'in your being taken straight out into the courtyard, blindfolded, and shot.'

"Captain Shagg caught the essential word 'shot,' and once more interposed.

"'Shall I draw?' he said. 'It's wonderful how reasonable a man'll get sometimes when you have got the draw on him.'

"'Keep quiet!' I urged. 'There won't be any shooting.'

"And I once more eyed the President carefully and took his measure.

"He hardly looked a coward. Beneath the manners of an attorney he probably concealed the natural ferocity of the average Spanish American. Unless the captain got the draw on him, and deterred him, it was conceivable (though not very likely) that he might carry out his threat. There was also the chance that he might be just obstinate enough to refuse to give way until the shells actually began to burst about his ears—which would have been awkward, as we had neither shells nor guns on board the little San Francisco trading steamer.

"Once more, therefore, it was necessary for me to modify my plan; and I modified it on the spur of the moment on lines suggested by my recent Nicaraguan experiences.

"'Your Excellency,' I began, 'our lives are no doubt in your hands. But the whole might of the British Empire is behind us, and if you lay a finger on us, you are putting your own head into the hangman's noose.'

"He was obviously frightened. But it still was not quite certain that he would give way. He might merely escort us politely to our boat, and then withdraw out of the range of shell-fire, leaving the buildings to take care of themselves. So I played the last trump card.

"'On the other hand, if we were alone, your Excellency,' I added, with the sort of smile that the Central American understands, 'if we were alone, I might be able to suggest——'

"He motioned to the soldiers to go and smoke their cigarettes outside, and then I spoke to him quite frankly, without troubling to wrap up my meaning in nice diplomatic phrases.

"'You're not President of this Republic for the benefit of your health, I take it,' I said. 'No. You've taken the Presidency for what you can make out of it. The salary is not large, but there are perquisites.'

"He smiled, beginning to catch my meaning, which I soon made absolutely clear.

"'Very well,' I continued. 'Your Excellency imagined, perhaps, that it was the intention of Her Britannic Majesty's Government to fine your country without recognising the service which you yourself have rendered. I hasten to inform your Excellency that this is not the case.'

"His Excellency's smile was now broadening to a grin.

"'My proposal is, therefore,' I proceeded, 'to increase the damages to the sum of 60,000 dollars—this sum to include a sum of 10,000 dollars by way of honorarium for your Excellency.'

"The President of the Republic of Salvador stroked his chin reflectively.

"'If you had said 75,000 dollars——' he began at length. I paused, weighed the point, and answered gravely.

"'Including 25,000 for your Excellency? It is a great deal. But I suppose I must strain the point—on condition, of course, that the money is brought to me immediately, and in cash.'

"'I was hoping,' said the President, 'that my own cheque for the amount——'

"'I said cash, your Excellency,' I repeated.

"'Or our notes? they are so much less cumbersome than our dollars.'

"'Cash, your Excellency. And it must be fetched from the bank and wheeled down to the quay for us at once.'

"'You drive a hard bargain, but I must perforce accept it,' said his Excellency.

"'And my gun'll cover the dagos in charge of it, by way of keeping them out of temptation,' said Captain Shagg. And then he clapped me on the back, crying——

"'Fifty thousand dollars to cut up between three of us! You're a dandy, stranger, you're a dandy!'

"But alas! his tone was different when, a few hours later, having steamed far away from the Port of Libertad, we had hauled down the Union Jack and assembled in his cabin to apportion the indemnity. For then he stamped upon the floor, and banged upon the table, and knocked the glasses over, and used words which I must not repeat.

"'Compose yourself, captain. What is it?' I inquired.

"'What is it? Why, in the whole of this pile of dollars there ain't one honest piece. I mean to say that they ain't the real thing, any more than your papers and my ship were. They're just struck to unload on gambling-hells. It's one of the industries of that cursed country.'

"It was my turn to be angry.

"'You knew that,' I cried, 'and you never warned me! You dolt! You thickhead! You unconscionable scoundrel!'

"My passion got the better of me. I flew at him, and we wrestled together on the floor, while the Vice-Consul whom we had rescued pointed out a better way.

"We wrestled together on the floor."

Stromboli and the Guns]   *[Page 160]*

"We wrestled together on the floor."

"'Listen to me! Listen to me!' he cried. 'I know the gambling-houses where they buy those moneys. I'll take you there to sell them! I'll get you a good price.'

"And so he ultimately did. He got us, in fact, a good deal more than we should have expected. But Captain Ulysses P. Shagg and Jean Antoine Stromboli Kosnapulski were never very good friends afterwards."

THE FRIEND OF THE POLICEMAN.

It was the morning after the Anarchist Club had been raided by the police. I was sitting up in my bed, reading the graphic account of the occurrence in the morning paper, when the door opened and Stromboli himself burst into my bed-chamber.

"Hullo!" I ejaculated. "So you have found bail! I was rather expecting that you would come to me for it!"

"I should have," was the reply, "if I had needed it."

"You did not need it? You mean that you managed to escape?"

"Precisely. Do I not know the tramp of a policeman when I hear it? Are not his boots made so that all the world shall know it?"

"Ah! then——"

"I was wise in time. Leaping on to a table, I shouted to my friends: 'We are discovered. This way for the back door. Follow me, and I will lead you to a place of safety.' Then I fled, and, as you see, I reached a place of safety. But alas! I reached it alone. The others, my followers, were caught. I weep for them."

"It is unnecessary," I explained. "The English law is lenient in these matters. A small fine will see them through their troubles."

My words failed to produce the comforting effect which I intended.

"If only I had known that!" Stromboli answered, and hung his head dejectedly.

"Yes? In that case?" I asked.

"In that case," he answered, "I should not have been in so great a hurry; and if I had not been in so great a hurry, I should not have left my purse on the piano."

"You did that?"

"I did that, having just taken it from my pocket for the purpose of paying for some refreshments. It contained the money which I had set aside for the satisfaction of the claims of my more pressing creditors. I shall have sleepless nights in consequence."

"So, I dare say, will they," I interposed; and the remark seemed to exhibit the situation to Stromboli in a light in which he had never previously looked at it.

"You really think so?" he answered sympathetically. "Then I am indeed distressed for them. I should have remembered that creditors as well as debtors might have their pecuniary embarrassments. If I could be of any service to them—if, for example, by telling another story——"

"Then you still know other stories?"

Stromboli jerked his head disdainfully, saying—

"If I know other stories! When I tell you that it was I who, at the time of the Commune of Paris—— But—voyons, mon cher—I have not yet breakfasted."

I took the hint and rang the bell.

"I thank you," said Stromboli. "I will have bacon and eggs for breakfast. It is a comestible of your country for which I have acquired a taste. Though I eat while telling you my story, yet I am an artist, and you may depend upon it that my mouth will not be full at any climax of my narrative."

"Then fire ahead!" said I, and Stromboli fired ahead, plying his knife and fork diligently while he unfolded—

THE ADVENTURE OF THE FRIEND OF THE POLICEMAN.

"You think it singular that a revolutionist should have feelings of friendship for a policeman? Singular it is, and only possible upon one condition—that the policeman's daughter is beautiful, and that the revolutionist is in love with her. I myself—I, whom policemen yesterday pursued through the kitchen and offices

64

to the back door, was at the time of the siege of Paris in love with the daughter of a *sergent de ville.*

"Her name was Fifine, and she was more beautiful than I can tell you—dark, with bright eyes, and a complexion like a peach in bloom, and the tender, coaxing manner which a man delights in. Her father, the Père Dubois, occupied an apartment in the same house with me at Montmartre; and as he was aware of my desire for the regeneration of the world, ferocious pleasantries used to pass between us.

"'*Voyons*, rascal!' he used to say to me. 'If it were not that Fifine would cry, I would march you straight off to the *depôt* and have you locked up there, so that you could do no harm.'

"'Old man!' I answered. 'If it were not that Fifine would cry, then I would pluck you by that nose of yours and drag you along the *boulevard*, an object of derision to all Paris.'

"'Name of a dog!' he retorted.

"'Name of a pipe!' I rejoined. And then I conciliated him.

"'Come now,' I said. 'For Fifine's sake, let us be friends. For Fifine's sake, let us swear a great oath, like the Homeric heroes, that if ever we meet in a battle, or even in a riot, we will spare each other.'

"The Père Dubois knew but little of the Homeric heroes, though he understood that they had distinguished themselves in the Napoleonic wars. None the less, he swore the oath over a good bottle of red wine, concluding philosophically—

"'Fifine is a good girl. I trust her. I shall tell her what to say to you, and she will reclaim you and make a good citizen of you yet.'

"To which I replied—

"'Père Dubois, you are very amiable. In compliance with your wishes, I will take quiet walks with Mademoiselle Fifine in the sheltered woods of the Buttes Chaumont, so that she may have every opportunity of converting me to your views. If the weather is fine, we will take such a walk to-morrow.'

"He grunted, but agreed. Perhaps, if he could have foreseen—but it is seldom given to a policeman to see as far into the future as a revolutionist. And now, perhaps, you picture Fifine imploring me with persuasive tears to turn my back upon the revolution and apply for a post in the *gendarmerie*! Then you do not know human nature; you do not know women; you do not know Jean Antoine Stromboli Kosnapulski!

"What is it that a woman likes in a man? She likes him to be different from all other men. She likes him to be strong and masterful, taking his own course and towing her like a little pinnace in his wake. If need be, she will even pique him to perversity; though, in my case, that necessity did not arise. So you must not be astonished when I tell you what Fifine actually said to me was—

"'How wonderful to be a revolutionist! Please tell me all about revolutions. I never met a revolutionist before.'

"She said it, clinging trustfully to my arm, while we walked together on the high, green hill of the Buttes Chaumont. All Paris was stretched out below us like a map. The blue smoke floated upwards from the chimneys in the autumn air. A misty haze obscured the view beyond the ramparts, and the booming of the big guns of Mont Valerien was the only sign of war; but from the streets ascended a confused hum of angry voices—the noise which, in Paris, expresses the discontent which the man of action can turn into a revolution almost by a gesture. In truth, it was high time for another revolution, and here was Fifine pressing me with her questions—

" We walked together on the high, green hill."

Stromboli and the Guns]   [*Page 167*

"We walked together on the high, green hill."

"'Please tell me all about revolutions. Please tell me what a revolution looks like.'

"Curious, is it not, that by such artless speeches women win men's hearts? One wonders if they know it. I answered, half in jest, while pondering a project in my mind—

"'A revolution, *amie chérie*? It is the simplest matter in the world. You get up in the morning feeling discontented, and decide that the Government must be overthrown. Other people are of the same opinion. You leap upon a *café* table and harangue them until you have stirred them to the depths of their souls; then you say, "To the Hôtel de Ville!" Some of you march thither, while others go into the churches and ring bells. The procession swells in volume; you call upon the soldiers to fraternise with you; the constituted authorities disappear through the back door. You write names on slips of paper and toss them out of the window. This is the list of the new Government. It is all over in the twinkling of an eye.'

"'How wonderful!' Fifine ejaculated, opening her eyes wide.

"A sudden idea came to me, and I acted upon it.

"'My angel!' I cried. 'I have told you what a revolution looks like. Now come with me, and I will show you one.'

"She looked amazed; it may be that she had reason to. It was such a chance as does not often come the way of the daughter of a *sergent de ville*. But I appealed to her curiosity.

"'Listen!' I said. 'You hear that noise?'

"She nodded.

"'Well, sweetheart,' I continued, 'whenever I hear that noise in Paris, I can turn it into a revolution in ten minutes.'

"'How wonderful!' she once more repeated.

"'Come and see,' I answered, and her curiosity prevailed over her years. We ran down the hill together, and in a few minutes were in the stormy streets of Paris.

"It was as I thought. The people of Paris were angry because the pinch of hunger was making itself felt. They were gathering in little knots, and someone was already haranguing them from a *café* table; but he was unworthy of the occasion, being drunk, so I pushed him down gently, amid applause, and took his place.

"'Why do we talk,' I cried, 'when the hour for action has arrived? The Government does nothing. Instead of driving away the Prussians, it deliberates. It is in no hurry, because it possesses secret stores of food; but we, in the meantime, what have we to eat?'

"'Rats! *En voilà un!*' one of my audience shouted, tossing a choice specimen across to me.

"I caught it dexterously and put it in my pocket. Then I went on—

"'You tolerate such a Government! You are willing that it should continue to rule you—to betray you! No, no! A thousand times no. You will sweep it away and govern Paris by yourselves. But there is no time to lose. To the Hôtel de Ville, my comrades! To the Hôtel de Ville!'

"Tame words, you may think, as I recite them to you now, in times of peace; but then they were burning words that caused men's blood to boil.

"'To the Hôtel de Ville!' the Belleville workmen echoed, and the mob became organic, and we marched.

67

"Imagine that march! Beginning as a small procession, it grew into a mighty mob, with red flags flying and a brass band playing; and at the head of it, Fifine and I walked, arm-in-arm. She was afraid, but she was curious; her curiosity was stronger than her fears. Ah, she was a true woman, was Fifine!

"'Oh! it is wonderful,' she kept repeating. 'I suppose it is wrong; but it is wonderful, all the same.'

"And no one laughed to see her. For those were sentimental days, when every revolutionist rejoiced to have a woman associated with him in his enterprise. It was as though some master of the ceremonies had said—

"'Your partners, gentlemen! Take your partners for the Carmagnole.'

"So we swayed on, in ever-swelling numbers, until the Hôtel de Ville was reached. A crowd was already besieging its doors and swarming up its stairs. It seemed, for the moment, as though I—I who had instigated this revolution—should be unable to get access to the building. But I called in a commanding tone—

"'Room there! Room for a lady! Room for Jean Antoine Stromboli Kosnapulski!'

"They fell back, as far as it was possible, and cleared a space for me. With Fifine still upon my arm, I jostled my way into the famous Hall of the Mayors. It took time, but at last we got there. Let me try and draw the picture for you.

"A large, long room, with portraits of celebrated citizens of Paris hanging on its walls. At one end of the room a large semi-circular table with the Mayors of Paris seated at it; the President in the midst of them, pale and indignant. The rest of the room packed with a crowd of revolutionists, women as well as men, all talking loudly at once, and a few *sergents de ville* among them, disarmed and overmastered, but unable to escape. And, struggling against the tumult, the rumour gradually spread itself from mouth to mouth—

"'The Breton Mobiles! They are coming to the rescue of the Mayors.' One saw the point of that. At all events, I saw it, even if the others did not. The Breton Mobiles understood no word of French—understood nothing but their own uncouth Celtic tongue. It would be useless to harangue them on the sacred right of insurrection and appeal to them to fraternise with people. They would sweep on, with fixed bayonets, driving the Parisians before them, blind, deaf, implacable as Destiny itself. For once in my life I perceived failure in front of me, and I felt that I owed Fifine an apology.

"'Dear angel,' I said to her, 'this is not so brilliant a revolution as I could wish, but it shall have its dramatic climax, all the same. Observe!'

"Then I continued to elbow my way to the front, exclaiming—

"'Room there! Room for a lady! Room for Jean Antoine Stromboli Kosnapulski.'

"The crowd parted as before, and I found myself close to the table of the Mayors, with the pale face of the President immediately in front of me. I pulled the rat out of my pocket and tossed it to him, saying—

"'Thanks to your incapacity, the people of Paris are eating rats. In the name of the Republic, I call upon you to eat a rat yourself.'

"The people who heard me cheered, but the Mayor of Paris tried to fling the rat back into my face. I caught it in my right hand and tendered it to him again with dignity.

"'Be reasonable,' I said. 'It is a present from Jean Antoine Stromboli Kosnapulski. As those English say, you must put the gift-horse in your mouth. In the name of the Republic, I call upon you to eat the rat before us all, and to pretend that you enjoy it.'

"A tremendous cheer broke from the assembled revolutionists. They shook their fists in his face and roared—

"'Let him eat the rat! Let him eat the rat!'

"He ate it, and we cheered him. Perhaps he was hungry, and needed it, for, owing to the disturbances, he had been a long time without refreshment; and though, to do him justice, he made little pretence of appetite, one of the women—a good, thrifty soul—could not resist exclaiming—

"'What a waste of a good rat! Why do you throw it away on him, when the people of Paris are hungry?'

"That, however, was a question which, in spite of its importance, I had no time to answer. At last the Mobiles were coming—the Breton Mobiles, with whom it was impossible for the Revolutionists to fraternise, because they did not know their language. There was no purpose to be served by staying any longer, the more especially as I had a lady in my charge.

"'Dear angel,' I whispered to Fifine, 'there is no more revolution to be seen to-day. I will make haste and take you home.'

"It was more easily said than done, but I was not a man to be deterred by obstacles. I shouted as before—

"'Room there! Room for a lady! Room for Jean Antoine Stromboli Kosnapulski!'

"And room was made. I myself helped to make it, by pushing vigorously with my strong arms. As the Bretons were entering by one door, Fifine and I were issuing by another.

"It was all over—for the time. Many arrests were made; but, in the confusion, Fifine and I escaped arrest, and it was not until the next day that I knew that my behaviour had been remarked by any public functionary. Then, however, I had a passage of arms with the Père Dubois.

"'Rascal!' he said. 'I saw you.'

"'How now? What do you mean, Père Dubois?' I asked.

"'I was in the Hôtel de Ville, disarmed and helpless. But I saw you, and now I go to denounce you to the Government.'

"I looked him straight and fearlessly in the eyes.

"'Remember your pact with me, Père Dubois,' I said.

"'My pact?' he repeated.

"'The pact we swore, like the Homeric heroes, that, even in a revolution, we would spare each other. This time, as the revolution has failed, it is I who am the gainer by it. Presently, when the revolution is successful, it will be your turn to profit.'

"His eyes fell before my gaze as he replied—

"'If it were not for Fifine's sake, I would not do it.'

"To which I answered—

"'If it were not for Fifine's sake, I would not ask you.'

"'You think, then,' he continued scornfully, 'that the day will come when it will be in your power to serve me?'

"'I am quite sure of it,' I answered, 'and when it comes, you may rely upon me. Let us shake hands.'

"So we shook hands, and an armed truce was restored between us; and the days rolled by, until the last great day came when I was called upon to fulfil my obligations.

"Most of the events of those days belong to history. You know how the Prussians at last starved Paris into surrender. You know how we Communists seized the reins of Government in the month of March. You know how Paris was besieged a second time, and how the barricades sprang up, and how there were bloody battles in the streets. I have nothing new to tell you of these things. I have only to tell you of the service which I, at the last, rendered to the father of Fifine.

"Fifine herself had been sent to visit friends in the country. Safe-conducts being hard to get, it had been necessary to lower her in a basket over the ramparts after nightfall. I well remember my last talk with her before, with no more luggage than she could carry on her arm, she disappeared into the darkness.

"'Sweetheart,' she said, 'I thought that revolutions were wonderful, but now I only find them terrible.'

"'Sweetheart,' I answered, quoting the proverb, 'how shall we make an omelette without breaking eggs?'

"That was too deep for her. She did not even ask whether the omelette was worth the broken eggs, but came to the point without either metaphor or simile.

"'Dearest,' she pleaded, 'I saw you begin the revolution. Can't you promise, for my sake, that you will stop it?'

"I shook my head sadly. It was hard for me, as you can judge, to confess that she had asked me a thing which it was beyond my power to do for her.

"'Dear angel,' I answered, 'the revolution is irresistible as the rising tide. A man may have the power to start it, but no man has the power to stay it.'

"'But my father!' she pleaded. 'Tell me! The revolutionists have no love for the police?'

"I was obliged to own, however regretfully, that they had not. For what have policemen ever done, that revolutionists should love them?

"'But, dear angel,' I added, 'one may make exceptions, if only for the sake of proving rules. I wield influence, as you have seen, and I will use it. They shall not hurt one hair upon the Père Dubois's head.'

"Then we kissed each other and said good-bye. Fifine disappeared, lowered over the ramparts by a sentinel; and it was only two days afterwards that the Versailles soldiers entered Paris, and the fighting in the streets began. I do not describe it to you. I do not boast. One brave man behind a barricade, I take it, is very like another. The tide of battle rolled us back from street to street. The traitors slunk away and hid themselves. The day came when we were only a handful of men, hemmed in by an army. Driven from my lodging in Montmartre, I found a garret to sleep in in Belleville. I was there, snatching the few hours' rest which I had earned, when a child found me, and thrust a note, hastily scrawled in pencil, into my hand.

"It was from the Père Dubois. How he had found the means of sending it I do not know; but this is what he said—

"'I am a prisoner of the Commune, locked up with forty other *sergents de ville* at La Roquette. Your Communists are murdering their prisoners. For the love of God remember your promise to me before it is too late!'

"My mind was made up instantly. Until then I had supposed that a prison was the safest place in Paris in which a *sergents de ville* could find himself; but since this was not so, I knew how to act.

"Springing from my truckle-bed, upon which I lay only half undressed, I put on my frock-coat and my silk hat, and knotted my red sash round my waist. Then I hurried down seven flights of stairs and almost ran into the arms of our leader, Citizen Ferré.

"'Well, Ferré, how goes it now?' I asked him.

"'Badly,' he answered. 'It is all over with us. The Versaillais press us hard. We have only just time to kill the prisoners.'

"At first I did not take him seriously.

"'Is that the way to raise the tone of revolutions?'

"He answered grimly—

"'Perfectly. We have dealt with the Archbishop; we have dealt with the *gendarmes*. If we make haste, we shall just have time to deal with the *sergents de ville*.'

"His brutal words horrified me, but I temporised. Time was precious, and I would waste none of it in wrangling. If it had only been the life of an ordinary hostage—an archbishop, for example—that was at stake, I do not say; but the life at issue was the life of the father of Fifine. Therefore, as I have said, I temporised.

"'You are right, Citizen Ferré,' I replied. 'We must indeed be quick. Let us see which of us can be the quicker. I will race you to the prison of La Roquette.'

"'Good,' he replied, and we both began to run with all our speed. Picture us; for the picture must indeed have been a strange one. The enemy surrounded us, and the crack of rifles and the screech of *mitrailleuses* sounded from the barricades on every side. The rival batteries on the Buttes Chaumont and the Buttes Montmartre hurled their shells all over Paris. Red flames and black clouds of smoke arose from the Tuileries, from La Villette, from the Hôtel de Ville, from blazing buildings in every quarter of the city. Dead bodies of men and horses lay here and there upon the pavements. Mattresses were piled up at the windows to serve as a screen against the bullets. And, in the midst of this, Citizen Ferré and I—he in his soldier's uniform, and I in my frock-coat and silk hat—raced each other to the prison of La Roquette. I was fleet of foot in those days, and I outstripped him. Dashing through the open gate in the prison yard, I called—

"'Where are the prisoners of the Commune? Where are the *sergents de ville?*'

"There was no need to ask the question. I could see the heads of several of them at the windows of the cells. So I continued—

"'I have the order for them to be shot. Let me go up to them and I will tell them to come down.'

"The words were saluted by a bloodthirsty cheer. It occurred to no one to dispute my authority or ask a question. The key was handed to me and I went up to the second storey and entered the door of the long corridor in which their cells were situated.

"'Gentlemen,' I began. 'I am Jean Antoine——'

"Before I could say more, a dozen strong arms had gripped me and thrown me on the ground, and my wrists were tied fast with a handcuff improvised from a piece of string.

"'A hostage! We also have a hostage,' they cried in an exultant chorus.

"Then, just as I was fearing more rough usage, I heard the voice of Père Dubois.

"'Be gentle with him. He is a friend of mine. Hear what he has to say.'

"So the policeman who was seated on my chest got up again, and I was able to proceed—

"'Gentlemen,' I gasped. 'Citizen Ferré is on his way here to have you shot. I raced him here that I might warn you. I am Jean Antoine Stromboli Kosnapulski.'

"They looked inquiringly at me and at each other, and in the meantime there came what looked suspiciously like proof that I was lying. Ferré had, at last, arrived, and a fresh messenger came to the entrance of the corridor; though, with greater caution than I had shown, he only spoke through the keyhole.

"'The order has come that all the prisoners of the Commune are to be released. Descend at once, and you can go free.'

"Some of them flashed a look of triumph on me, seeming to expect that I would blush for shame. But I did not blush. I sprang up and stood with my back to the door, and retorted hotly—

"'Idiots! Are you taken in, then, by a simple trick like that? It is a lie to get you down into the courtyard, and shoot you the more easily.'

"This gave them pause.

"'There's reason in that,' they said. 'No doubt the hostage knows the nature of the Communists. But what to do?'

"I was impatient.

"'What to do?' I shouted. 'Do you want a revolutionist to tell you what to do? Barricade yourselves, idiots. Barricade yourselves, and stand siege till the Versaillais come.'

"Their good sense prevailed; they jumped at the suggestion.

"'It is an idea; let us barricade ourselves. Untie the hostage's hands, that he may help.'

"It was done, and I, who had shown the people how to build so many barricades in the streets, now taught these forty-two policemen to build a barricade in the corridor of the prison of La Roquette. We made it by taking the mattresses from the beds in the cells, and laying them one upon another carefully and symmetrically, as one builds a wall with bricks. The barrier was so high that no one could climb over it; so thick that no bullet could pass through it; so solid that it could only be pulled down, piece by piece, by unmolested labourers; and scarcely had we finished it before we found the need of it. We heard the voice of Citizen Ferré himself, no longer promising safe-conduct or immunity.

"'Since you won't come out of it by yourselves, we'll have to fetch you out. Charge, my lads, charge, and we'll treat them as we did the *gendarmes* in the Rue Haxo.'

"Hurling themselves against our woollen wall, they tried to push it before them by sheer weight. It did not yield an inch. Was it not built by a revolutionary leader? And were there not forty-two *sergents de ville* supporting it with their weight upon the other side?

"'Pull it down, bit by bit, from the top, then,' Ferré shouted; and we heard a noise as of a man being hoisted on to another's shoulders, and, for an instant, had a glimpse of a villainously ugly face between the barrier and the ceiling.

"But only for an instant. Père Dubois—he also hoisted on to a neighbour's shoulders—hurled at the man a piece of crockery intended for a very different purpose. It smote him full upon the jaw, knocking teeth down his throat. Swearing a terrible oath, he disappeared, and no one took his place. Carried away by the joy of battle, I shouted to the Communist, who had so lately been my friend and ally—

"'Citizen Ferré! Is this the way you raise the tone of revolutions?'

"'Pig! We are not beaten yet,' my old friend answered; and, as we heard him retreating down the staircase, we wondered what fresh devilry he had in his mind.

"Presently we heard a fresh noise above our heads. Somebody was breaking through the ceiling. Armed though we were, after a fashion, with cudgels and lances, which we had made by breaking up the woodwork of the beds, we knew that we could not hold out long against an assault from that place of vantage. There seemed nothing to be done save to sell our lives as dearly as we could.

But, just as we had made up our minds to this, we heard a voice that reassured us.

"'Hush! Do not be afraid! We are your fellow-prisoners.' And the head which revealed itself through the broken planks—the head at which Père Dubois was preparing to hurl a fresh piece of crockery—proved to be the head of one of the parish priests of Belleville, whom the Communists had locked up as their hostages. The *sergents de ville* greeted him with shouts of welcome.

"'Listen!' said the good old man. 'We have barricaded ourselves, and shall fight for our lives if need be. But, in the meantime, as your lives also are in danger, we would strengthen you with our prayers and with our blessing. Kneel, my brothers, kneel.'

"We knelt. It was a strange ceremony—such a ceremony as has never been, perhaps, in the world, before or since. There was no confession. The time was precious and too short for that. But, as we fell upon our knees and bowed our heads, the holy man solemnly pronounced absolution and chanted benediction. Even I—Jean Antoine Stromboli Kosnapulski, of whom priests in a general way do not approve—took absolution and benediction with the rest. Then the cry was raised—

"'Look out! They are returning!'

"We went to our post again, wondering what fresh device our enemies had hit upon. It was not long before we knew. They had released the convicts—the thieves and murderers who had been in prison long before the Commune made special prisoners of its own—and had enlisted them as willing allies against their natural enemies, the *sergents de ville*. We heard them fraternising in the yard.

"'Long live the Communists!' cried the one.

"'Long live the convicts!' replied the others.

"And then, once more, we heard the brutal voice of Citizen Ferré—

"'Now, pigs! Your hour is come. Since you won't come out any other way, we're going to burn you out.'

"In another instant they had poured petroleum over our mattress barricade and set light to it. It burnt slowly, for wool, packed close, is but a poor combustible, and there was no draught to coax the flames. The whole corridor, however, was filled with a suffocating stench. We coughed and choked, though we had burst every window open. It was only a question of time. Our barricade must ultimately yield to this attack.

"'Water! Oh, for water!' was the cry that went up on every hand. We had no water save the filthy stuff in which the prisoners had washed, over and over again, since their cells had last been cleaned. So far as we could, we soaked the mattresses with these slops. They added to the stench, but hardly helped to quench the fire. With luck we might hold out for half an hour. Longer we could not hope to hold.

"The *sergents de ville* were losing heart and energy. They had thrown themselves on the floor, because the smoke was less there, and lay about the passage like so many dying men. And Père Dubois whispered to me—

"'Oh, think of something! For Fifine's sake, think of something!'

"An inspiration came to me. I ran to the window, braving the risk of rifle-bullets, and put my head out of it, and shouted with all my might—

"'The Versaillais! The Versaillais! Hold out! Hold out! I see the Versaillais coming!'

"The effect was marvellous. The *sergents de ville* leapt to their feet again. The convicts scurried down the staircase, tumbling over each other in their haste. They streamed out into the courtyard and became a frightened mob. Their terror was contagious, and every man sought to save his skin. They peeped cautiously through every open door, and when they saw the coast clear made a run for it. They fetched ladders out of unexpected places and scaled the prison walls with them. Citizen Ferré himself attempted to swarm up a water-pipe.

"And there were no Versaillais coming. I had invented them because I saw that they were necessary to save the situation. They did not actually come until more than two hours afterwards; though, in the meantime, we saw nothing of my old friends, Citizen Ferré and his companions.

"At last, however, the little men with the red trousers came marching into the courtyard, and I said—

"'Let me go down and explain. The Colonel will be surprised to see me.'

"Well might he be surprised, even though he failed to recognise me. My frock-coat was singed and torn; my silk hat was battered, and the nap on it was ruffled; my face was as black as a negro's from the smoke. I must, indeed, have looked a pitiable object as I issued from the door, exclaiming—

"'Welcome, M. le Colonel. I am Jean Antoine——'

"A bullet splashed against the wall beside me, and I withdrew. Tearing off my red sash, and borrowing a helmet and a tunic from one of the *sergents de ville*, I reappeared and resumed my friendly greeting.

"'Welcome, M. le Colonel. Herewith I restore to you forty-two policemen whom my old friend Ferré would have shot. I have raised the tone of revolution. I am Jean Antoine Stromboli Kosnapulski.'

"I bowed profoundly, and this time no rifle-bullets interrupted my discourse.

"The Colonel merely said—

"'Whoever you are, you'll remain under arrest while the truth of your story is inquired into.'

"'That, M. le Colonel,' I said, 'is only reasonable. I am sorry that I have no sword to surrender to you. My only weapon has been a piece of crockery. If you wish that it should be formally handed to you, I will go and fetch it.'

"He did not wish it, but proceeded to try me by drum-head court-martial on the spot. With what result you can conjecture. A prisoner who has forty-two policemen vying with each other to give evidence in his favour has little to fear even from an improvised military tribunal.

"In consideration of my services to the police I was dismissed, within two minutes, without a stain upon my character, and even thanked for what I had done to raise the tone of revolution.

"To think that, after that, I should have lived to be chased by policemen, as I was yesterday, through the kitchen and offices, out of the back door! Fifine, my angel Fifine! what would you have said if you had lived to hear of it?"

THE SECRET SOCIETY.

There is no more mysterious, and no more misrepresented society than the Camorra. I never understood its nature or its objects until I heard Stromboli's story. He went to Naples and discovered the Camorra. He investigated it and found out exactly what manner of society it was. But let him tell the story in his own words:—

"I had no sooner come to Naples," he said, "than the Camorra forced itself upon my notice. Even as I landed from the steamer, I observed the boatman who had brought ashore my modest luggage surreptitiously slipping a small coin into the hand of a stalwart bystander, gaudily attired in the costume that one associates with brigandage, who had all the air of accepting it, not as an alms, but his due. My watchful curiosity was at once excited.

"'Who is that man, then?' I asked the sailor curtly.

"'It is the Camorrista, signor—it is the Camorra man, sir,' he answered, in matter-of-fact tones, as he lifted my luggage into a carriage.

"I began to wonder.

"My carriage rattled over the stones and set me down in my hotel. Another stalwart individual was waiting there. He, too, was an ornamental person; he wore wide velvet breeches with gold lace upon them, a loose white shirt, a red sash, and a gaudy silk handkerchief knotted over his head. And he, too, reached out his hand to claim a coin which my driver dropped into his palm.

"'Who is that man?' I asked again, and got the same answer as before—

"'It is the Camorrista, signor—it is the Camorra man.'

"'And why do you give him money?' I inquired further.

"'Because he demands it, signor,' the man replied; and he jumped on to his box and drove away before I had time to pursue the subject any further.

"I went on wondering.

"Evidently this was a strange country to which I had come—a country in which you had only to demand money in the name of a mysterious society in order to obtain it. Would people also give money to me, in case of need, if I also dressed gaudily and stepped forward with a bold address, saying 'I am the Camorra man'? The question furnished food for thought.

"'To-morrow,' I said to myself, 'I will investigate this matter. In the meantime, I will dismiss it from my mind, and dine.'

"I ceased wondering, therefore, and ate my dinner, and strolled out into the city to divert myself.

"My diversion took the form of a game of billiards in a *café*, which was not, I must admit, one of the most fashionable *cafés* in the city. It was, in fact, a *café* in the dark and narrow street known as the Tre Capelle—the street of the Three Hats. There was a better opportunity of observing the life of the people there than in the more fashionable quarters.

"But I did not merely observe the life of the people. I also won the people's money. My skill at billiards was not, in those days, inconsiderable. In several successive games I was the victor, and each game was played for a higher stake than the game preceding it. Altogether, perhaps, I won enough to pay my hotel bill for a week. Then I pocketed my profits and bade the company a courteous 'Good evening.'

"'*Addio!*' I said, waving my broad-brimmed hat and smiling; and then took my umbrella—for it had been raining—and stepped jauntily into the street.

"Hardly had I gone half-a-dozen steps when a stranger stepped out of the shadow and approached me.

"The street was dimly lighted with oil lamps, and I could not see him well, but I saw that he, too, was gaudy and robust. His small round felt hat had cocks' feathers in it, and he wore earrings which glittered in the lamplight. He brandished a cudgel in his right hand, while his left was extended like a mendicant's.

"'Our share, signor?' he asked peremptorily, if not quite truculently.

"'Whose share? And whom may I have the honour of addressing?' I retorted with no less determination.

"'*Il Camorrista*—the Camorra man,' he rejoined, in just such accents as he might have used had he been able to announce himself as the policeman on duty in the neighbourhood.

"A sudden curiosity seized me. How would this imperious man behave, I wondered, if I were to prod him quite suddenly and very violently in the pit of the stomach with the point of my umbrella? It seemed an interesting experiment, and one well worth trying.

"'Here, take your share!' I cried, and lunged at him with the skill and rapidity of one accustomed to the foils.

"My eye and aim were sure, and the result was satisfactory. The ferrule struck my antagonist just beneath the breast-bone—at that sensitive point, in fact, which your prizefighters always aim at.

"He uttered a cry of pain, staggered, doubled up, and fell in a heap upon the ground.

"'*Addio, Camorrista*—farewell, Camorra man,' I said, and strode away with dignity, to the amazement and admiration of the onlookers.

"But my experience had interested me. I felt that I had lighted upon a mystery, and I was resolved to probe it to the bottom. To that end I rang my bedroom bell the next morning and put a question to the chambermaid who answered it.

"'Tell me, Lucia, what is the Camorra?'

"She stared at me as blankly as though I had requested her to define space or time.

"'What is the Camorra, signor? The Camorra, signor—it is the Camorra,' she replied.

"It was an inadequate explanation, but I thought I might succeed better if I tried a gentler method. So I kissed her and took her hand caressingly.

77

"'*Voyons*, sweetheart!' I said. 'There is no need for you to be afraid. I will protect you. Tell me everything that you know about this Camorra.'

"To my amazement, she snatched her hand away and ran screaming down the corridor.

"I changed my tone.

"'*Voyons*, baby! Send up the landlord to me!' I shouted after her.

"He came with the indignant air of a man whose establishment I had outraged by the commission of an impropriety; but I received him with an indignation equal to his own.

"'*Voyons*, landlord!' I exclaimed. 'What is the meaning of all this? Is this house a lunatic asylum?'

"He replied that it was nothing of the kind.

"'It is because my house is not a lunatic asylum,' he added, 'that I invite the signor to leave it without delay.'

"It was natural that I should express myself strongly.

"'Leave your house!' I said. 'Neither your manners nor your macaronis tempt me to make a long stay in it. But before I go, I must have an answer to a question. I insist. Attend!'

"He glared, as though knowing that the question would be an awkward one. I met his gaze and put the question firmly.

"'What I want to know is this: What is the Camorra? Why have I been invited—unceremoniously and with menaces—to subscribe to it? To what purpose would my subscription have been devoted had I paid it instead of felling the agent of the society—the collector of its tribute—with an unexpected blow?'

"But I did not get the plain answer to the plain question which I thought I had a right to. Nor did I get admiration for my courageous feat of arms. My landlord's face expressed only amazement and dismay. He threw up his arms with the gesture of a man abandoning hope.

"'The signor struck the Camorrista?'

"'I have already told you that I struck him with great force, to the astonishment of the spectators. I left him in the gutter of the street of——'

"'Then the life of the signor is in peril, and my life also. The vengeance of the Camorra——'

"'What is this Camorra, then?' I interrupted.

"'The Camorra is——"

"'Well?'

"'The Camorra is the Camorra. It is forbidden to say more.'

"'But I command you to say more.'

"My tone—perhaps my movements also—implied a vague threat of violence. But the landlord did not wait for me to lay hands on him. He fled, as the chambermaid had fled; but he slammed the door after him and turned the key and locked me in. Then he called through the key-hole—

"'Will the signor forgive me? It is the only way. I will arrange for the signor's safety before the Camorra——'

"I heard no more, for I was hanging on to the knob, rattling the door, and kicking at the panels.

"They would not yield, being solid, as though built in the old days when any house might be required at any time to stand a siege. I assailed the door, first with a chair, and then with a wash-hand jug, with no result except that I broke both of them. Then I sat down and reflected. My window was on the fourth floor and looked on the hotel courtyard, so that escape in that direction was impossible. But there still remained one other plan. I had my revolver.

" I assailed the door, first with a chair."
Stromboli and the Guns]   [*Page 201*

"I assailed the door, first with a chair."

"'Stand clear there, everybody, while I shoot!' I called through the key-hole; and then I pulled the trigger and blew away the lock.

79

"In the silence which followed the report I heard the tramp of heavy footsteps in the corridor. Still gripping the smoking weapon, I stepped outside to receive my visitors.

"Imagine my surprise when I saw that they were policemen, and that my landlord was guiding them to my apartment, carrying the key. His language was polite, however, and he offered an explanation.

"'It is arranged,' he said. 'If the signor will be so kind as to pay his bill, these gentlemen will afford the signor the protection that is necessary for him.'

"'And the Camorra?' I asked.

"'Hush!' he replied, lifting both his hand to enjoin silence.

"So I paid my bill and accompanied my police escort, trying to think more kindly of my landlord.

"'The good man means well,' I said to myself. 'He fears lest I should be assassinated by this terrible and all-pervading society. He procures me police protection. I will write to him and say that it was quite unnecessary, but that I am nevertheless obliged to him.' Then, as we got out into the street, I proceeded to enter into conversation with my escort.

"'*Voyons!*' I said to them. 'You, at least, my friends, will be able to give me some information about this mysterious Camorra.'

"'Silence!' in authoritative accents was the only answer that I got.

"'Have a glass of wine with me, then, before we go any further,' I suggested.

"They agreed to that, and sat round me outside a *café* and drank at my expense; but the refreshment did not make them much more communicative. The Camorra was the Camorra. It was secret; it was powerful. It helped its friends, and punished its enemies without mercy. The people who did not belong to it had to pay tribute to those who did. That was all the information I could get.

"'It must be a society that works for the revolution,' I suggested.

"'Silence!' came the answer again, in accents half savage and half scared; and we left the *café* and marched on.

"It occurred to me that we had gone far enough, and that I did not need police protection any longer. I said so, adding:

"'Where are you taking me, my friends? To the railway-station, or to the steamboat?'

"They laughed. It is not often that a policeman laughs, but these policemen laughed like countrymen at the theatre seeing their first farce.

"'Where are we taking you?' they cackled, with horrible grimaces.

"'Precisely. That is my question?'

"'Well, to the prison, of course. Where else?'

"'To the prison, indeed! But I am under police protection!'

"They roared with laughter.

"'Under police protection! It is a way of putting it, when one has a light heart and loves a joke.'

"'A joke'?"

80

"'Certainly, seeing that you are under arrest.'

"'On what charge?'

"They shrugged their shoulders like one man.

"'Who knows? There may be a charge; there may be none. It may be sustained; it may break down. Who knows?"

"'Do you mean to tell me that at Naples a stranger may be arrested——'

"'Obviously.'

"'With no more ceremony than if he were being asked to dinner? I do not believe it. There is some mystery here. The Camorra——'

"'Silence!'

"'The Camorra is at the bottom of this. The Camorra and the landlord are in a conspiracy against me——'

"'It is possible. We have no information on the subject.'

"'But I will resist their machinations. I will confound them. I will probe the mystery to the bottom. I am Jean Antoine——'

"'It is possible—we have no information. But here is the prison.'

"Resistance was out of the question. It seemed likely, indeed, that I should be safer in the prison than outside it. There, at least, I might find some intelligent person who would listen to my explanation; there, at least, I should have respite from the attentions of the Camorra, and a plain answer to a civil question.

"Patience!" I said to myself, as the great gate clanged behind me; and it soon became evident that I should have need of patience. For this Neapolitan prison was quite different from any other prison that I had ever been confined in.

"There was no ceremonious reception of new-comers by the authorities; they did not even trouble to ask who one was.

"There was no privacy. Separate cells were only provided for prisoners condemned to death—a heavy price to pay for such a privilege. For the rest, the inmates were herded together in great courtyards, with no distinction between those convicted and those awaiting trial, and no one, so far as I could see, to supervise their conduct. It was, as it were, a republic of evil-doers in which I was turned loose to take my chance and find my level.

"'There are your quarters. Soup and macaroni are served out twice daily. The other prisoners will tell you where you can sleep,' said the gaoler curtly.

"'But I demand to know——' I protested.

"'Silence! Don't bother me with your foolish questions,' he replied, and slammed a door and disappeared.

"So I got no satisfaction from him, and my heart sank within me. A period of *ennui*—a term of weary waiting, with discomfort but without excitement—that seemed to be the fate in store for me. But once more—so far, at least, as the excitement was concerned—I was mistaken. A fellow prisoner provided me with immediate excitement.

"He was tall, lithe, masterful in demeanour. He approached me, like the man whom I had prodded in the stomach after my game of billiards, with one hand extended for a donation, and the other brandishing a cudgel.

"'The due?' he demanded curtly.

"'What due?' I asked calmly.

"'To buy oil for the lamp of the Madonna.'

"It was a formula, though I did not know it. But I was not, as you may suppose, in a conciliatory temper. I drew myself up haughtily and said: 'My good man, I was not aware that I had the pleasure of your acquaintance.'

"He introduced himself.

"'*Io sono il Camorrista*—I am the Camorra man.'

"It was a blow to me. Were my footsteps to be dogged there, even in prison, by the representatives of this mysterious society? It seemed so. Yet, in a sense, I was glad to meet it there. It was a chance of solving the perplexing mystery, and I determined to solve it, even at the risk of a temporary misunderstanding.

"I fixed my eyes on the man, showing that I was ready to defend myself, and spoke to him seriously.

"'*Voyons!*' I said to him. 'The last Camorra man who was rude to me is now suffering from a pain in the pit of the stomach, and he wasn't either so rude or so ugly as you are.'

"'*Corpo di Baccho!*' the man exclaimed, making as though he would strike me, yet hesitating before my determined attitude.

"'But let us be reasonable,' I continued. 'Let me make a proposal to you.'

"'Speak!'

"'Ever since my arrival at Naples, I have been curious to know what your Camorra is, and what it does with the money which it collects with such systematic industry. If you will tell me, I will give you a piece of gold; and if you do not tell me, I will give you nothing.'

"Would he have yielded if we had been alone? I cannot say. A knot of our fellow prisoners had gathered round us, and his pride was at stake.

"'Silence! You have not to ask questions, but to pay.'

"My temper was roused, and I resolved to precipitate the crisis. I flung a piece of gold—part of my winnings at the billiard-table—on the ground, and challenged him.

"'*Voyons!*' I cried. 'No one shall say that Jean Antoine Stromboli Kosnapulski is mean. There is your money, and I will fight you for it.'

"A fierce cry of approval went up from the bystanders.

"'A duel! A duel!' they exclaimed in chorus, and the representative of the Camorra—to do him justice—did not shrink from the encounter.

"'Antonio!' he called to a companion, 'fetch knives!' And I made the strange discovery that, in a Neapolitan prison, the prisoners were allowed to borrow knives for the settlement of their affairs of honour.

"But I would not have a knife. It is a weapon in the use of which I have had little practice.

"'No, no!' I cried. 'I will take no unfair advantage of you. It shall be your knife against my umbrella. Does that seem fair to you?'

"He seemed to hesitate, as one who dreads an unfamiliar danger; but the public opinion of the prison was in favour of my proposal. It had novelty; it promised strange spectacular effects calculated to relieve the tedium of prison life. So my opponent found it impossible to refuse.

"'As you prefer,' he said; and seconds were appointed and a space was cleared. At the given word, we advanced to meet each other from opposite corners of the court-yard.

"Do not ask me for details of the combat! I am not vain. Therefore I will not dwell upon them at undue length.

"It was like this. The Camorrista at first advanced stealthily, with long, catlike strides; and I on my part advanced firmly, holding myself upright, like a master of fencing of the French rather than the Italian school. Then the Camorrista launched himself upon me like the greyhound bounding upon the hare. I saw his purpose—to grip the stick of my weapon with his left hand while he lunged with the right with a quick, simultaneous movement. As he seized it, I thrust at him, taking a quick pace to the right as I did so. He fumbled and was delayed for half a second, and the delay gave me my chance. As soon as my right foot was planted on the ground, I launched the *coup de savate* with my left. Before he could swing the knife round, and at the moment when he was bending slightly forward, the blow caught him in that same point beneath the breast bone in which my antagonist of the previous evening had been wounded.

" As soon as my right foot was planted on the ground, I launched the
coup de savate with my left."

Stromboli and the Guns]   *[Page 21]*

"As soon as my right foot was planted on the ground, I launched the *coup de savate* with my left."

"The knife dropped from his grasp. He fell moaning and helpless. It was over. I was victorious; and I pointed with my umbrella at my opponent where he lay.

"'*Voyons*, gentlemen! The coin remains my property, I think,' I said, picking it up and replacing it in my pocket.

"'If any other gentleman desires to do battle similarly for the Madonna's oil,' I continued, but none came forward. On the contrary, they cheered me as the ancient Romans, of whom you have heard, might have cheered a triumphant gladiator.

"'I thank you, gentlemen,' I said, bowing with dignity, and walked away.

"But my triumph was to have a consequence which I did not foresee. For the remainder of the day my mind was not entirely easy. Some of my fellow prisoners were whispering together in a manner that did not tend to reassure me. My antagonist had partially recovered and was the centre of mysterious conclaves. There seemed reason to fear that an advantage would be taken of me while I slept—some act of violence done to me in the dark.

"'*Voyons!*' I said to myself. 'I cannot keep awake every night; but this night it is necessary that I should watch and see what happens.'

"Nor had I long to wait before I saw something to justify my fears. The very man whom I had discomfited in the morning was creeping stealthily towards me along the dormitory floor, where I lay stretched, as all the others were, upon a poor, hard mattress. I waited until he had got quite close to me, and then suddenly sat bolt upright, with my hand on my umbrella, prepared to strike with it. But there was no need to strike.

"'Hush!' the man whispered. 'You proved yourself this morning. I now come to you as a friend. I bring you these.'

"Imagine my surprise when I saw him gently place a small handful of small coins upon my bed.

"'What does this mean, then?' I whispered in reply, still watching and suspecting treachery.

"'It is your share.'

"'My share of what?'

"'Of the *barattolo*—of the funds that we collect.'

"'But——'

"'It is offered as a token that we wish you to be one of us.'

"'One of you? One of the Camorra?'

"'Precisely. It is the rule, when a man has proved himself, that he shall be invited to be one of us.'

"It really seemed as though my chance had come to get an answer to my question. I reached out my hand in sign of amity and asked it.

"'Speak to me as a friend, then. Excuse my ignorance, and tell me what is this Camorra which I am asked to join.'

"But I was once more put off.

"'Hush! It is the rule only to inform the companions by degrees.'

"'But you might at least begin informing me?'

"'Yes, I may tell you something. It is a society—secret and powerful. Those who do not love it, fear it. It has influence everywhere. It brought you here. It will arrange you your release to-morrow, by withdrawing the charge against you. A companion will meet you at the prison gate. Do as he bids you.'

"'But the object of the society? The purposes to which it devotes the great sums of money which——'

"'Hush! It is of that that I must not inform you yet. You know, at least, that it is better to be the friend of the Camorra than its enemy.'

85

"And that, at any rate, was clearly true. Can you blame me if, knowing that, and desiring my release, I agreed to join the society even without a full knowledge of its objects? Can you blame me if I further felt that loyalty bound me to be obedient to the behests of the companion who was to await me at the gate? This time I had to do with a Camorrista dressed as a gentleman.

"'You are the new companion?' he asked me, when I came out.

"'I am the new companion, Jean Antoine Stromboli Kosnapulski,' I replied.

"'I was expecting you,' he said.

"'It is very kind of you,' I answered. 'Perhaps you will add to your kindness by informing me what are the political objects of this interesting society in which I have enrolled myself.'

"'Hush!' he said. 'At present I am only permitted to inform you of the duties which you are to discharge.'

"'Your behaviour strikes me as very equivocal,' I protested.

"But he reasoned with me gently.

"'What!' he said. 'You would know all—before you have proved yourself, before you have given guarantees? You will not trust the Camorra even when the Camorra shows that it has trust in you? Consider, now. Does not our confidence merit yours?'

"'But I have a curiosity to know.'

"'Naturally—most naturally. And it will not be very long before your curiosity is gratified.'

"'How long, then?'

"'A week, perhaps.'

"'You mean that?'

"'Most assuredly. There are men who have worked years to conquer the privilege which you have won by a single act of courage.'

"'In a week, then——'

"'In a week you will receive notice of the meeting called for your initiation as a member of the Camorra.'

"'And then I shall know all?'

"'All—provided that in the meantime you have faithfully performed the duties that I lay upon you.'

"'Your words are plausible,' I said. 'You are an honest man. Let me shake hands with you.'

"We shook hands, and my colleague explained the nature of my appointed task. Outside the *café* at which I had felled the Camorrista to the ground, I was myself to stand as the representative of the Camorra. I was to collect the Camorra's share—a tenth of every winner's winnings. I was to account to the Camorra for the money—the Camorra would dispose of it.

"'It does not strike me as an occupation of great dignity,' I represented.

"'Indeed! It is a position of trust that I assign to you.'

"There clearly was something in that.

"'If I were quite sure,' I added, 'of the objects of the association, and of the use to which the money would be put——'

"He smiled and nodded, saying—

"'You will soon know; and when you know, you will have no reason to be displeased.'

"Then he left me, and I lunched and proceeded to my post, and acted to the best of my ability as Collector of Revenues to the Camorra.

"There were no difficulties to be encountered. The tax-collectors of the Government must have envied me the simplicity of my task. There were no troublesome forms to be filled up; there were no irritating requests to call again. I had merely to extend my hand, and the coins were counted into it without demur. Nor had I to keep books. To prevent mistakes, I put the Camorra moneys aside in a separate bag. For the rest, there was perfect reliance on my honour.

"In due course a letter was slipped into my hands, running thus—

"*Dear Companion,—It is for to-night, in the cellar of the house by which thou watchest. Thou shalt be initiated, and then shalt be informed of all. Nothing further.*

"'THY COMPANION.'

"It was a great occasion for me, and I prepared myself to do full justice to it.

"'*Voyons!*' I said to myself. 'I will make my toilet; and while I am making my toilet, I will compose my speech. *Grande tenue*, I take it, will be *en règle*. Even if I am wrong, I shall have paid my companions a compliment by thinking so, and it will also be a compliment to be able to address them in a few well-chosen words.'

"So, as I had no dress-clothes with me, I hired a suit, wearing also a flowing cape to cover it, in case it should seem ostentatious; and I collected my thoughts and polished my phrases, that I might deliver a suitable harangue, on the principles of whatever revolution might be contemplated.

"Alas! it was a waste of energy, as you shall see. Listen to me, I beg of you, while I describe my first and last appearance at a formal committee meeting of the Camorra.

"The place was a long, low room, below the level of the street, reached from the *café* by a winding staircase; stone oil-lamps, swinging from the ceiling, lighted it dimly, clouds of tobacco smoke thickened the atmosphere; bottles of red wine and tumblers were set out on a long table on which no cloth was laid.

"There were from twenty-five to thirty companions present—companions of all kinds and all social grades; companions who had all the appearance of prosperous professional men—doctors, lawyers, and magistrates—some of these, like myself, were in evening dress, with white gloves; companions who looked like working men; companions who looked like wandering Neapolitan mandolinists. It seemed strange that *camaraderie* should prevail among them; yet so it was. They sat round the table together clinking glasses, while I was placed on a high stool near the door awaiting the ceremony of my initiation. It was a very simple ceremony. The president of the assemblage rose and addressed me.

"'It is the rule,' he said, 'to require a new companion to prove himself by fighting a duel with some existing member of——'

"'I shall be most pleased,' I interposed. 'If you yourself, Signor President, will do me the great honour of encountering me, I will endeavour——'

"'In certain cases,' the president continued, 'the rule is waived. It is waived in your case, because you have already proved yourself.'

"'On two occasions, Signor President,' I reminded him.'

"'Precisely—on two occasions. Consequently the third proof is not required.'

"'You are quite sure, Signor President? I ask no favour. Rather than that any irregularity should be committed——'

"'There will be no irregularity. It will only be necessary for you to swear the oath. Repeat it after me.'

"He recited the formula, a short and simple one. I swore to be faithful to the Camorra, to keep its secrets, to obey its orders, to betray no companions to the police. And that was all.

"'Now drink,' said the president. And a tumbler of red wine was handed to me, and I duly drained it to the dregs, after first walking round the table and clinking glasses with every member.

"'And now,' the president continued, 'we reach the business of the evening.'

"I listened eagerly. At last, it seemed, the mystery was to be solved, and I was to learn the secret of the Camorra—in what sacred cause it gathered in its revenues, and by what subtle means it proposed to employ them for the overthrow of principalities and powers. The truth burst upon me like a thunderbolt.

"'Giovanni, bring me the books!' called the president to a subordinate. And two great ledgers, such as you see in merchants' offices, were laid before him.

"'And the cash!' he added; and a number of small bags full of coins were also brought.

"In a few minutes he was immersed in calculations, while a loud buzz of talk went on around him. Then he looked up, and banging upon the table, called for silence. When he spoke, you could have heard a pin drop.

"'The week has been a fortunate one,' he said, and cheers broke out. 'In addition to the ordinary tribute collected on the quays, at the hotels, and in the *cafés*, some heavy fees have been received from farmers whose cattle the companions have promised not to poison, and from citizens at whose houses the companions have undertaken that there shall be no burglaries. The *barattolo*——'

"'*Viva il barattolo!*' shouted the companions gleefully.

"'The *barattolo* for the week amounts to the sum of 20,000 lire (loud cheers). When the necessary deductions have been made for working expenses, and for the remuneration of the office-bearers of the society, there remain 730 lire for each companion.'

"Not a word, you perceive, about the political purposes of the society, concerning which I had been promised information. I rose from my stool to point out the omission.

"'*Voyons*, companions——' I began, but the president signed to me to be silent and continued—

"'Let me proceed to the distribution of the funds. Giovanni, take this bag first to the companion, Jean Antoine Stromboli Kosnapulski.'

"My turn had come, and I was free to speak. They cheered me as I rose, imagining, no doubt, that I wished to return thanks for the honour done to me. But this was not my purpose. My suspicions were awakened, and I concentrated those suspicions in the form of searching questions.

"'This bag of money is for me,' I began.

"'Naturally,' replied the president.

"'To do what I like with?'

"'Absolutely.'

"'And for each companion present there is a similar bag for him also, to do what he likes with?'

"'Assuredly. We are all brothers here.'

"'And the great revenues of this great society are collected for no other purpose than to be thus divided weekly among the favoured few?'

"'Precisely. For what other purpose should we trouble to collect them?'

"'Then I have a word to say.'

"For now the truth was out, and my suspicions were confirmed, and indignation had followed in their train.

"The companions stared at me—puzzled by my vehemence; but I quickly made them understand. The burning sentences flowed like red-hot lava from my lips. The speech which I delivered was not the speech which I had prepared. It was an infinitely greater speech.

"'Yes, I have a word to say to you; and that word is this. You have deceived, deluded, fooled me, you have inveigled me by your fair words into a companionship of which I find myself at once ashamed.'

"A murmur was arising, but I quelled it.

"'Silence! I have not finished. I have but begun. By your nods and your winks and your mysterious words you led me to believe that in joining you I was joining the mightiest revolutionary society that the world had ever seen. Heaven knows that I shrink from no revolutionary enterprise. Heaven knows that I am willing to adopt strong measures to raise the money which such enterprises need. And I thought that you were raising money for such a purpose, and that I was helping you to raise it. But what do I find? I find that you plunder—plunder the poor and weak and helpless—not for a cause, but for yourselves. I thought to be taking part with you in a high political conspiracy, and I find myself—I, *moi qui vous parle*, find myself—sitting and drinking in a den of thieves.'

"There was a further murmur; but this, too, I quelled.

"'Silence! I have nearly done. It remains for me to shake the dust from off my feet. It remains for me to say that I resign my membership, that I repudiate you, that I sever my connection with you, that I denounce you——'

"But I got no further. It was the word 'denounce,' unfortunately chosen, with its suggestion of betrayal to the police, that spurred the companions to action. Their numbers gave them courage; their knives flashed; as a single man they leapt at me.

"It was no time for argument. I hurled my stool at the nearest of them, and so secured a start. On the winding stair one of them clutched at the skirt of my cape; I threw my arms back, so that it came off in his hands. Then, in my evening dress and opera-hat, I gained the streets and ran, some twenty Neapolitan ruffians, with their knives drawn, pursuing.

"'It was no time for argument. I hurled my stool at the nearest of them.'"

Stromboli and the Guns]   *[Page 225*

"'It was no time for argument. I hurled my stool at the nearest of them.'"

"But I was fleet of foot, and they pursued in vain; and when I had reached the railway-station, and jumped into the carriage of a departing train—which seemed, in the circumstances, the safest place of refuge—I found that my bag of coins was safely in my pocket.

"'*Voyons!*' I said to myself, as I examined it. 'If I could return each of these coins to its rightful owner! But that is obviously impossible; there is no alternative but to retain them as a memento of a remarkable experience that is hardly likely to occur again.'"

THE VISIT TO THE HOLY MAN.

It was at the time when the name of the Senussi—the mysterious Holy Man who frightened the Foreign Office from an oasis of the Libyan Desert—was in the papers.

"The Senussi!" exclaimed Stromboli. "When I tell you that I—*moi qui vous parle*—have spoken with the Senussi; when I tell you that I—*moi qui vous parle*—have inflicted an indignity upon the Senussi; nay, more, when I tell you that the Senussi and I exchanged indignities! Are you at leisure? Then let me tell you."

I consented to listen; and Stromboli began—

"You all talk of the Holy Man with bated breath, as if he was Beelzebub; but I, for my part, always spoke of him openly and fearlessly. And it happened one day, some fifteen years ago, that I was imparting information about him to some old friends of mine, who were Irish members of your House of Commons.

"'He's a holy man and a strong man,' I was saying, 'and he gets holier and stronger every day, and he knows how to bide his time. One day, when he's holy enough and strong enough, he'll get up in the middle of the night and preach the Holy War. And then beware! His followers will come out of the desert like a swarm of locusts and eat up the country.'

"Having made this speech, I proceeded to withdraw with dignity; but one of the gentlemen followed me down the stairs, and spoke to me in an Irish accent—

"'Oirish whisky, Mr. Stromboli,' he said, 'is better f'r y'r health than the Scotch that ye've been drinking, an' I happen to know a little place round the corner...'

"I accepted the invitation as cordially as it was given, never guessing that it was the prelude to a political proposal; but the refreshment was no sooner set before us than my companion broke the ice.

"'I was listenin' just now with very much interest to y'r conversation, Mr. Stromboli. Ye were spaking of a sartain holy friend of yours.'

"'Hardly a personal friend,' I corrected.

"'Ah, well! ye said he was a holy man, and a powerful man, and ye seemed to know a good deal about his ways. So it occurred to me, between ourselves, to make a little proposal to ye.'

"It seemed to me, at this stage of the proceedings, that I had better ask my friend his name.

"'Me name?' he replied. 'Well, of course, that's what I should have begun by telling ye. Me name's Biggar. Maybe ye've heard of me. I'm a member of the Irish Nationalist Party.'

"I bowed; while Mr. Biggar took off his spectacles, wiped them, put them on again, and peered at me with his penetrating little eyes. Then he called for further glasses of whisky, and proceeded—

"'Well, now ye know me name an' me position in life, and we'll proceed to business. What I was about to ask ye was whether ye think it loikely that this holy friend of yours could be persuaded to take up the cause of Home Rule for Oireland.'

"I pointed out the obvious difficulty—that the Holy Man was a Mohammedan, and that the Irish people were not; but Mr. Biggar was not disconcerted.

"'I've thought of that, sorr,' he replied. 'I was thinking of that over the first glass of whisky; and the way out of the difficulty is now clear to me. All that ye have to do is to put it to the Holy Man in this way—that the down-trodden Oirish people are prevented from becoming Mohammedans because they have not yet obtained Home Rule.'

"I congratulated Mr. Biggar on the ingenuity of his argument, and he advanced it a step further.

"'I'm thinkin', Mr. Stromboli, that the party to which I hold the confidential position of treasurer might perhaps make it worth y'r while to pay a visit to Mr. Senussi.'

"'*The* Senussi,' I corrected.

"'Ah! So they say The Senussi, just as we say The O'Donoghue. It's a further bond of union between us. And as I was saying, I'm thinking it might be made worth y'r while to go and see him, and present him with me compliments—the compliments of Mr. Joseph Gillis Biggar—and suggest to him that he should create a diversion in the direction of Egypt, at the time when the Oirish members are moving the adjournment of the House of Commons. Will ye tell me now what ye think of the proposal?'

"I looked him in the face to make sure that he was sober and in earnest. I saw that he was both, and raised no objection when he called for a third glass of whisky.

"'*Voyons*! Mr. Biggar,' I said. 'This is a very dangerous mission on which you propose to send me. Are you aware that the oasis in which the Senussi lives is surrounded by Arabs who have absolutely no other work to do except to murder all strangers who approach it without satisfactory credentials?'

"But Mr. Biggar was not confounded by the question

"'That's what I was thinkin' of over the second glass of whisky, Mr. Stromboli,' he replied; 'and I have already thought out a plan for you.'

"'Unfold it, Mr. Biggar,' I said. And he unfolded it.

"'It's like this, Mr. Stromboli. In addition to bein' an Oirish member, I'm in business, as ye may have heard, as a provision merchant.'

"'Proceed, sir,' I said; and he proceeded.

"'There's one of me customers that's a Mohammedan. He's an Arab who throws raw potatoes into the air and catches them on the bridge of his nose and breaks them, in circuses in the North of Oireland; but he doesn't pay up very easily, and I've threatened to County Court him for his bill. Now I'm thinking that it w'dn't take a great deal of persuasion to induce that performing Mohammedan to give ye the sort of letter of introduction that ye require.'

"And Mr. Biggar called for a fourth glass of whisky; while I pointed out a further difficulty—that a Mohammedan who wrote from Ireland might perhaps fail to inspire the Senussi with confidence.

"'I was thinkin' of that over the third glass, and it's no difficulty at all, at all,' said Mr. Biggar. 'The man w'dn't date his letter from the circus, and he w'dn't mention that he made his livin' by catchin' praties on the bridge of his nose; he'd date it from just where ye like, and he'd say just what ye please in it. Now, Mr. Stromboli, are ye satisfied? Take a minute or two to think it over.'

"I reflected for a minute or two with folded arms. Then, having made up my mind, I gripped Mr. Biggar by the hand.

"'Mr. Biggar, you are a man of genius,' I exclaimed. 'Jean Antoine Stromboli Kosnapulski says it. There now remains no difficulty but one—the payment of my travelling expenses in advance.'

"His expression changed, as I have heard that it always did when money had to be disbursed; and his tone, for the instant, was almost unfriendly. At any rate it was peremptory.

"'Now, mind me,' he began. 'Ye'll go thurred class, and ye'll take some packets of sandwiches so that ye needn't be always dining in the hotels, and ye'll——'

"But I overawed him.

"'Mr. Biggar,' I said. 'Pray observe that you are not speaking to one of your Irish members. You are speaking to Jean Antoine Stromboli Kosnapulski.'

"'I ask y'r pardon, sorr; I ask y'r pardon,' said Mr. Biggar.

"'It is granted,' I replied with dignity. 'The brusqueness of your manner is no doubt necessary with Irish members, when they are at once indigent and exigent; but your heart is in the right place. And now, with your permission, we will discuss the details of our project.'

"'While I have been drinkin' me fourth glass,' rejoined Mr. Biggar, 'it has occurred to me that that will be the more profitable course. General principles are best agreed upon over the convivial bowl; but it would be an error of judgment to settle the practical minutiæ while under its influence, the more especially as the good people here are now engaged in turning out the lights.'

"So we bade each other an affectionate farewell, postponing the adjustment of the details, which were duly arranged at other interviews conducted in the day.

"I need not dwell upon them. Suffice it to say that my travelling expenses and my letter of introduction were both forthcoming in due season, the latter being written at my dictation, and checked and corrected, for the prevention of treachery, by an eminent Oriental scholar. As for my remuneration—

"'We'll pay ye by results,' said Mr. Biggar; 'and ye'll find that ye'll be treated very handsomely on the day when Ould Oireland gets Home Rule.'

"And his parting speech was—

"'Me bhoy, ye're one of the broightest jewels in the crown that Ould Oireland's foightin' for, and I'm only sorry we can't be after givin' ye a public dinner by way of a send-off. But there's the danger that the Holy Man would come to hear of it, and shoot at ye from behind a hedge in the desert, just for all the world as if ye were a landlord. So ye'd best go about the business stealthily. And now good luck to ye.'

"So we shook hands on the platform at Charing Cross, and I set forth alone upon my perilous adventure.

"My starting-point was Cairo. There I was to hire camels and guides, and buy presents to propitiate hostile chiefs; and there began my pilgrimage across the wide and burning wastes of the Libyan Desert.

"You will not ask me for particulars of that desert journey. One journey through the desert is very like another—blazing days and chilly nights; a parching thirst that no drink really quells; the sandstorm blown along by a wind like a blast from an oven; the welcome rest beneath the date palms at the wells; the glorious sunsets that seem to set the heavens aflame; but no real incident unless you miss the wells and die of thirst, or marauding Arabs find you out and fall on you, and slay you, or drive you away to be sold in some slave-market in the heart of the dark continent.

"And I—*moi qui vous parle*—I braved those terrors, protected only by my Arabic letter, written at my dictation by the degenerate Mohammedan who broke raw potatoes on the bridge of his nose in the circus in the North of Ireland.

"Again and again my guides tried to persuade me to turn back, their terror increasing with every step that took us nearer to our destination.

"'To draw near to Jarabub is forbidden,' they said; 'Senussi-el-Mahdi will slay us, and our blood will be on our master's head.'

"I retorted with emphasis and even with temper.

"'Are you not under my protection, and have I not paid you in advance? Go to, then, and lead on. Otherwise, your blood will truly be upon your master's head, here and now. For I will slay you, and leave you for the crows to pick your bones."

"'It is fated,' they said, and moved on sulkily.

"But presently I saw that they were whispering together; and I guessed what they were planning—to murder me in the night-time and steal away. Against this danger also, therefore, I took precaution.

"'*Voyons!*' I said. 'You have the souls of slaves, and like slaves shall you be treated. This night, and every night, shall you sleep bound, so that you may not run away.'

"But, to my amazement, my proposal did not make them angry.

"'So be it,' they said. 'For then will Senussi-el-Mahdi know that we are indeed our master's slaves, and that it is our master alone who is accountable and worthy to be put to death.'

"So I tied them up—none the less securely because they had professed themselves willing to be tied—and, so to say, drove my guides before me towards the Oasis of Jarabub.

"Once or twice parties of Arabs, springing, as it seemed, out of the yellow sand, came upon me in the early morning, and bade me turn back to the place that I had come from.

"'It is the will of Senussi-el-Mahdi,' they explained, 'and he cares but little whether we send thee back or slay thee where thou standest. Turn back, therefore, dog of a Christian, lest a worse thing befall thee.'

"No doubt they would have killed me without parley, if they had not seen that I was armed and could retaliate. But I had my rifle in my hands and two revolvers in my belt, so that they listened to me, or, rather, to my guide Abdullah, who interpreted.'

"'Nay, but we come as friends,' Abdullah said, 'and our master bears a letter for Senussi-el-Mahdi from a true son of the Prophet in a distant land.'

"'Son of a dog, thou liest!' said the savage and discourteous Arab.

"There was nothing for it, therefore, but to show him the letter and let him read it. He still seemed only half convinced, but that sufficed.

"'It is strange,' he said, 'but Senussi-el-Mahdi, who knows all things, will decide, when he has put thee to the question. It may be that he will make thee welcome, and it may be that he will slit thy throat; but I must not slit it for him until I know his will. In the meantime hast thou not perchance some gift for me?'

"I unpacked a burnous from my baggage and handed it to him with a courteous inclination.

"He took it from me with as little ceremony as though it had been a contraband article detected at a custom-house; but he made a sign to his men, and they melted away as suddenly as they had come in sight.

"We hurried on, starting each morning before dawn, so as to travel quickly while the air was cool, until one day, when the dawn broke, suddenly almost as a flash of lightning, the gleaming walls of a city showed themselves in front of us.

"'It is Jarabub,' said my guides with a single voice, throwing themselves upon the ground to say their prayers.

"I told them to make haste with their devotions and come on; and in half an hour or so we had reached our goal, and were seeking admission at the city gates.

"Do you ask me to describe the city? Well, I should say that, from a distance, it looked not unlike a group of disused limekilns, and that the resemblance did not entirely disappear when one got close to it. But I had no time just then to observe it closely. The walls and the windows were crowded with black men dressed in white, and bawling questions in a language that I did not understand.

"It was my luck that there was a man in the crowd who knew the English language; for then I knew what line to take.

"'*Voyons!*' I said to myself. 'A black man who knows English knows also Englishmen, and is accustomed to be ordered, and not asked to do what is required.'

"And to him I said, in the tones of one accustomed to command—

"'Hi, you, there! What's your name, and where do you come from?'

"The effect was instantaneous, as, indeed, I had expected. Old memories and associations triumphed, and he spoke to me as a black soldier servant to his officer—

"'Kroo boy, sah, from West Coast, sah. Name Bottled Bass, sah. Hope you quite well, sah. Get you plenty chop one time, sah.'

"It was the perpetuated triumph of the higher civilization over the lower. I lost no time in following it up.

"'That's all right, Bottled Bass,' I said; 'we'll see about the chop later on. Meanwhile get this gate open, and tell Senussi-el-Mahdi I want to see him. Say I've got a letter from an old friend of his at Mecca.'

"To an Arab, of course, I should not have spoken thus; but it was clearly the proper way to speak to Bottled Bass. The Arabs themselves seemed favourably impressed on finding that I spoke to this recent negro convert with less ceremony than to themselves; and he himself seemed proud to be spoken to at all.

"It was not likely, of course, that he would be in a position to convey my message personally. But he was a friendly interpreter, and he would pass it on. Exclusive though the Senussi might be, the rumour would reach him, and his curiosity would be aroused. And so it happened.

"After a pause the city gate was opened, and I was allowed to enter. I was put in a courtyard, closely guarded, and given some dates and a jug of water. The population came and stared at me. But, at last, after weary hours of waiting, a message was delivered to me. Abdullah and Bottled Bass were jointly charged with its interpretation.

"'The unbeliever is summoned to the presence,' was Abdullah's rendering.

"'This way, sah. Follow the gen'leman, sah,' was the gloss of Bottled Bass.

"The momentous hour had come, and I will not pretend that I approached it without apprehension. But there was no trace of nervousness in my demeanour. I was grave and dignified. Knowing what was due to myself, as well as what was due to my host, I met Senussi-el-Mahdi in the manner in which one high potentate meets another. It is not my fault that his attitude towards me was less courteous.

"Let me give him his due, however. He was a man of imposing and remarkable appearance: tall, with a fine full beard flowing to his waist, yet not hiding the fact that his chin was square and resolute; keen-eyed, as one who read the hearts of those who come before him; slow, but very masterful in his gestures. Save for his dress—he wore loose white robes and a turban on his head—he might have reminded one of those old-fashioned English schoolmasters at whose least word boys trembled. One would not dare to jest with him. He spoke French as well as Arabic.

"I bowed to him most ceremoniously, but he did not return my bow. It was a bad beginning.

"'What would you with me?' he asked curtly; and I explained myself.

"'I have come from a far country,' I said, 'that the light of Senussi-el-Mahdi may shine upon me. I am Jean Antoine Stromboli Kosnapulski.'

"He merely stared at me as at some strange insect.

"'Yes,' I repeated, 'I am Jean Antoine Stromboli Kosnapulski, and I bear a letter which will in part explain the reason why I seek this interview.'

"He motioned to a guard, who took the letter from me and placed it in his hands. He read it aloud, translating it for my benefit into French—

"*From Mohammed-ben-Ali of Mecca, to the most Holy Son of the Prophet, the Chosen of God, Senussi-el-Mahdi. Greeting.*

"*With my own hands I write to thee commending to thee one who dwelleth among unbelievers yet worshippeth Allah according to his lights, and journeyeth to thee that a fuller light may shine upon his heart. Instruct him in the truth, O Mahdi! and he will be thy faithful servant. Nay, more, when instructed by thee in the Book, he shall in his turn instruct thee how the light may be spread among a people who yet live in darkness because their rulers hide the light. He is a man of a stout heart, moreover, and will draw the sword for thee at the hour when thou proclaimest the Jehad.'*

"Senussi-el-Mahdi read this calmly and without visible emotion. There was no outburst of cordiality such as I had hoped for; there was no outburst of anger such as I had feared in the event of his guessing that I had come to him with forged credentials. Perhaps he had some faint suspicions; perhaps he was only following the ordinary rule of procedure in such cases. I cannot say. I only know that his manner was cold and judicious—like that of a schoolmaster to whom a new boy has been brought to be examined.

"'You are sent to me for instruction? It is well. Speak, then, and tell me if thou knowest the Koran.'

"It was a question that I was not prepared for, but I blurted out an ambiguous answer.

"'I know a little of most things, and my memory is good. As for the Koran, I know a very good translation of it, on which the skilled opinion of a scholar of your eminence——'

"'So thou knowest not the Koran,' interrupted Senussi-el-Mahdi pitilessly. 'Or shall I question thee therein?'

"This, too, was a proposal which I had not anticipated. It is not impossible that my face may have shown signs of my confusion. I stammered out the only excuse that occurred to me—

"'I have had a long journey, and am tired. With rest and preparation—

"But once more Senussi-el-Mahdi stopped me.

"'It is well,' he said. 'Thou knowest not the Koran. But thou hast asked for instruction, and thou shalt be instructed. When thou hast learnt the Koran, I will hear thee further on the subject of the letter.'

"And he motioned to the guards, saying—

"'Conduct him to the school, and place him in the lowest class.'

"Need I say that things were happening by no means as I had intended them to happen? Need I add that the word 'instruct' would never have appeared in my credentials had I surmised that it would be interpreted so literally? Yet it is clear, I think, that at the moment no useful alternative to doing as I was told was open to me. So I followed my guides.

"No violence was used to me; no harsh words were spoken; though I must have been a puzzle to the inhabitants, they were too well disciplined to show it—all of them, that is to say, except Bottled Bass, who grinned at me with gleaming teeth.

"They showed me to the room that I was to live in. It was close to the residence of the Senussi himself, who wished, I suppose, to keep an eye on me. And then they put me to school. I—*moi qui vous parle*—a man of much general knowledge and wide experience of life, was put to school—and in the lowest class! I had to sit, cross-legged, in the midst of a semicircle of negro boys, while a learned Arab, with a stick and a manuscript, sat in the centre and taught.

"'No matter,' I said to myself, 'my time will come, and I will bide my time, and earn my promised fee.'

"But I was curious to know the term of my probation; and I put the question to my teacher as politely as I could.

"'In view, sir,' I said, 'of the zeal for knowledge which I am demonstrating, would you mind informing me how long this interesting course of instruction is to last?'

"'You are as a little child,' he answered kindly, 'but it may, be, if Allah wills it, that in seven years you will have acquired the knowledge of a man.'

"Seven years of this tomfoolery! It was too terrible! My heart sank and my temper rose—the more so when I perceived that Bottled Bass, who was also a member of the lowest class, was grinning; and I retorted hotly—

"'Do you take me for a fool, then? A little Koran is all very well in its way; but seven years of it! If you can't shorten the course considerably, sir, I'll get up and walk out of the place!'

"The teacher answered, more in sorrow than in anger, that my words should be laid before Senussi-el-Mahdi. He went out to report them, and presently returned, and said, still more in sorrow than in anger—

"'El-Mahdi says that it is written that you shall be chastised, in order that you may learn humility.'

"And, almost before I knew what was happening, my teacher had motioned to two tall serving-men, and they had laid me on my back, holding my feet in the air, and the good old man himself was caning the soles of my feet.

"I know not whether the pain or the indignity was the worse, for both were very great. But the pain passed and the indignity remained. The more I reflected on the matter, the more certainly I felt that my position in the sacred city was untenable. Neither for the cause of Ireland nor for my promised fee would I consent to sit for seven years learning the Koran, and being caned when I displeased my teacher.

"Yet how to get away—that was indeed a knotty problem to think out. My teacher himself, who bore me no ill-will, but had merely punished me for what he considered to be my good, told me, in the kindness of his heart, that it would be impossible to get away.

"'Though thou shouldst take the swiftest camel in the city,' he said, 'yet wouldst thou be overtaken. For among the gifts of God to Senussi-el-Mahdi is this gift: he throws himself into a trance so that none can wake him, and his dreams are messages that flash across the desert, and become answering dreams in the brains of other faithful followers of the Prophet. Thus would he speed word of thy escape, and the faithful would lie in wait for thee and bring thee back. Wherefore be comforted, for it is written that thou shalt stay with us, and become, in the fulness of time, a holy man.'

"This time I did not answer hotly, having learnt from experience that it would be better not to do so; but I withdrew to meditate.

"'*Voyons!*' I said to myself. 'Let me think things out. Surely I have thought out things as difficult in other days!'

"And so I gradually framed my plan, examining it and adding to it nightly while I lay awake. This is how the plan slowly built itself—

"'Shall I slip over the wall and get away at night? It might be done, but it would be of no use. I should only be in the desert, where I should die of thirst. Shall I steal a camel? But one cannot steal a camel quite so easily as one can steal a cat or dog—nor can one lift a camel over a wall at night. What then? There is no way of going without Senussi-el-Mahdi's leave.'

"Thus I began thinking; and as night succeeded night my thoughts took more useful shape.

"'How to get leave to go? If I could lay Senussi-el-Mahdi under some great obligation—but that is hard. He is not the man to be sensible of obligations. He will let me go only if he can be made to feel that it is to his interest to be rid of me.'

"That narrowed the problem. But how to prove to Senussi-el-Mahdi that it would be well for him to let me go? It took at least three weeks' hard thought to settle that; but, at the end of the three weeks, light flashed upon me.

"'*Voyons!*' I cried. 'He has trances, and when he is in a trance——'

"I did not dare to speak aloud the thought that was in my mind; but I nursed it, filling in the details, and waiting patiently.

"As I have told you, I slept in a room quite near Senussi-el-Mahdi's own, and I now made it my rule every night to creep on tiptoe to his chamber and peep through his curtains to see whether his sleep was a trance or not. Night after night I crept back disappointed. But the night came at last when I saw that he lay stiff and still, with his eyes wide open and yet seeing nothing; and I knew that at last the hour for action had arrived.

"'He will either murder me or let me go,' I said to myself. 'I will take the risk. It is the only way.'

"With that I crept back to my own room, and fumbling in the dark among my belongings, found my razor. I looked out of the window to make sure that no one saw or heard me; but the city was silent, save for the dismal howling of stray dogs, and the watchman pacing on the walls. Then I lit a tiny lamp, and covering it with my hand, crept back to where the Senussi lay.

"To murder him? A poor plan that in a city where every man would be eager to avenge his death. To threaten him? He was hardly a man who would keep a promise made under the influence of threats. I had a plan that promised better.

"'It is a great art, the barber's!' I whispered to myself, as I mixed the lather and plastered it gently on his chin.

"He did not wake; he did not even stir. His soul was far away, communing with the souls of other pious Musselmans elsewhere; and while it wandered, I— *moi qui vous parle*—shaved Senussi-el-Mahdi where he lay.

"To what purpose? You will begin to grasp my purpose when I describe the manner in which I shaved him.

"For I did not shave him altogether; nor did I shave him precisely as the barbers shave. Far from it. On the contrary, I shaved off the beard on the right side of his face and the hair on the same side of his head; and then I took cosmetics and twisted out his great moustache until it stretched six inches or more either way, like furious spikes of straw.

"'Now for a looking-glass,' I said to myself; and having found a mirror, I so fixed it that, when Senussi-el-Mahdi woke, he would look straight into it and see his altered image.

"To what purpose? Surely you have guessed. But I had not yet quite finished my strange task.

"'*Voyons, mon cher,*' I went on, soliloquising: 'I think I should like your portrait as a souvenir.'

"So I crept back once more and fetched my camera, and blew magnesium powder through the flame of the little lamp to make a flash-light, and took my snap-shot of Senussi-el-Mahdi in his trance.

"The flash aroused him from his slumbers. His eyes opened, and he saw the reflection of his face. Doubtless he would have yelled in his amazement, but I took a quick step forward and clapped my hands upon his mouth.

"My self-possession and my quick wit had now returned to me. I was no longer the schoolboy, humbled and chastised. I was Jean Antoine Stromboli Kosnapulski, master of the situation. My tongue was loosened, and my words flowed quickly.

"'You know me?' I began. 'I am Jean Antoine Stromboli Kosnapulski.'

"Senussi-el-Mahdi nodded his grotesque head slowly. Half his proud spirit seemed to have left him with the loss of half his hair.

"'You have trampled on me,' I continued, 'you have insulted me; you have inflicted shameful indignities on me. But no man with impunity treats Jean Antoine Stromboli Kosnapulski thus; and now my hour has come.'

"A menace was rising to his lips; but I had only to hold the mirror once more before him to subdue him. As I have said, his self-confidence forsook him when he saw how ridiculous he looked. I continued—

"'You have made me speak to you humbly as a pupil to his master—as a sinner to a saint. But that is over now. I have treated you with ignominy, even as you treated me; and now that account is squared between us, I speak to you as man to man.'

"'Dog of a—' he began; but once more I held the mirror to him, and he changed his tone, and merely asked—

"'What would you have with me, then?'

"'Listen,' I replied. 'I know well that you have but to speak the word to have me slain. But I know also—and you, too, know—that, if you speak that word, the reputation of Senussi-el-Mahdi is for ever lost. Think of it, then! A Mahdi with half a beard and half a head of hair, and a waxed moustache like a Hungarian hussar's! The thing is too ridiculous! It could not be.'

"And once more I emphasised my criticisms with the mirror; and he looked at me with impotent rage, and did not speak.

"'Listen,' I continued. 'You can keep your holy reputation only if you hide your shame by veiling yourself until your beard has grown again; you may even acquire an added holiness. Who knows? But you can only keep your secret if you let me depart from Jarabub in peace. What say you, Holy Man?'

"He still seemed to hesitate; but this time I had merely to point to the mirror to decide him.

"'Depart in peace,' he said.

"'But I shall need guides and an escort,' I replied.

"'You shall have them.'

"'And a letter of safe conduct. Take your pen and write.'

"I put the materials before him, and he wrote at my dictation:—

"'*Senussi-el-Mahdi to all whom it may concern. Greeting—*

"'*Jean Antoine Stromboli Kosnapulski, the stranger within my gates, goeth on a high errand for me to Cairo. Let him have guides and camels. Let him start at once. Protect him and speed him on his way.*'

"'Good,' I said; but then I remembered something else.

"There were his trances, and the murderous messages that he might send in them. Against that risk also I must make provision. So I made him add—

"'*Take warning, also, that there is a certain false prophet, an enemy of the stranger, who sendeth messages in my name. Haply he will send false messages compassing the stranger's death. Know, therefore, that such messages come not from me; and slay any man who seeks to harm one hair of the stranger's head. And in the meantime, let none disturb me for two days.'*

"'Now sign it,' I said. And Senussi-el-Mahdi signed; and having gained my end, I once more treated him with courtesy and consideration.

"'Farewell,' I said. 'May Allah make your hair and beard grow quickly! For your hospitality—such as it was—I thank you. Rest assured that I shall guard at least one pleasant recollection of my sojourn here.'

"With that I bowed several times, and walking backwards respectfully, gradually left the room.

"And so—as I had no trouble in the desert—my adventure ended happily.

"My fee, indeed, is still unpaid; but I have not ceased to hope for it. Even now the Sect of the Senussi agitates and causes trouble; and many Irish members, having made wealthy marriages, are in a position to recompense, with interest on the over-due account, the service rendered them by Jean Antoine Stromboli Kosnapulski."

THE END.

CPSIA information can be obtained at www.ICGtesting.com
Printed in the USA
LVOW11s0049020414

379826LV00019BA/971/P